Tears Of A Princess

Laura Thomas

Publishers Note:

This is a work of fiction. All names, characters, places, and events are the work of the author's imagination. Any resemblance to real persons, places, or events is coincidental.

Cover Art: Val Muller

ISBN 13: 978-0615859781
ISBN 10: 061585978X

DWB PUBLISHING
CHILDRENS LINE
www.dwbchildrensline.com

For my Mum and Dad—

Who lovingly raised four "princesses" and taught us we are daughters of The King...

~ One ~

The summons had been direct.

Natasha was to report to the living room upon her arrival home. Since both parents were waiting for her, it must be something serious. Natasha had the feeling this was going to be bad.

Surely they hadn't discovered her secret, had they? She was so very careful covering her tracks. She knew they didn't understand the pressure she was under… nobody did.

Natasha sank deeper into the passenger seat of the car and wished she could stay there forever. Charlie, their part-time chauffeur, pulled the BMW around to the front of the house and briskly jumped out, surprising for his age.

Waiting for him to open the passenger door, Natasha's eyes roamed over her mansion of a home. How could something so magnificent, in one of the most prestigious areas of San Francisco, be so uninviting? It boasted perfectly manicured lawns, expertly crafted landscaping, and impeccable home décor—the finest of everything for the Smithson-Blair family. She snorted. Theirs wasn't a family—who was she trying to kid?

"Thanks, Charlie," Natasha said with a sigh, sliding gracefully from the car.

"You're very welcome, Miss," Charlie replied in his usual chipper way. He closed the door behind her and stopped in his tracks. "You sure you're okay, Miss? You don't look quite yourself this afternoon, if you don't mind my saying."

Natasha smiled at the grandfatherly man. He had worked for them for several years and drove for her grandparents before that. In some ways, he was more like family to her than her own flesh and blood. Charlie survived many of Natasha's temper-tantrums and mood swings in her early teens and always sensed when something was wrong. He was the only one who could get away with uninvited prying.

"I'm just tired, Charlie—we had extra ballet classes today, and now I've been summoned by the parents to top it off. But I'm okay, really. You go on home and have an awesome weekend."

Charlie took off his flat cap and scratched his balding head. "Try not to worry, they're most likely planning your sixteenth birthday celebration or something. What you need is to get some meat on those bones. Enjoy your family dinner and I'll see you bright and early on Monday for school. Bye, Miss."

Natasha forced a smile, picked up her dance gear, and took a deep breath. Head held high, she turned from the car, marched passed the spouting water fountain, and entered the place she dreaded most—home.

Turning the key and pushing open the ornate front doors, Natasha entered the foyer, slipped off her tan, leather boots, and dropped her bag on the travertine tile. There was no smell of dinner cooking—Maria, the housekeeper, must have the night off.

Just as well, I wouldn't have eaten anything anyway.

Instead, the overpowering scent of vanilla candles wafted through the house.

Shaking off her leather jacket, Natasha threw it over a velvet chair. With a weary groan, she glanced at her reflection in the enormous mirror.

Why do we have so many mirrors in this wretched house?

Natasha sucked in her stomach and smoothed several stray wisps of hair into her ballet bun, before making her way toward the formal living room. With the three of them in this huge space, they very rarely came together anymore, which made today's meeting especially ominous.

"Natasha, darling, we're waiting for you." Georgia Smithson-Blair had a voice that could saturate an auditorium without effort, yet never came off as being loud. It was smoothly cool, demandingly silky, and incredibly annoying.

"I'm right here, Mother, no need to bellow." Natasha was a match indeed for her mother's volume.

Natasha entered the living room and glanced at her father sitting uncomfortably in one of the leather wing chairs. She enjoyed being a daddy's girl—his princess. She loved him fiercely and knew that he was a very powerful and highly respected man in his sphere of financial business. However, William Smithson-Blair always seemed to shrink in the presence of his wife, and that bothered Natasha. If only *he* would fill the room for once.

"Can we get this over with?" she whined. "I've been dancing all day and I'm in desperate need of a nice, hot bubble bath."

There was an uneasy shift in the atmosphere and both parents hesitated momentarily.

"Natasha, please sit down, darling." Georgia patted the space beside her on the cream sofa. Natasha obeyed, too physically drained to do otherwise.

She noticed her mother's turquoise dress was new. It clung perfectly to her trim, toned body and made her tan look even more gorgeous than usual. But uncharacteristically, her mother's Botox-enhanced forehead was furrowed. She wondered when she had last seen an imperfection on that face.

"Tasha." Her father suddenly came to life and leaned forward, elbows on his knees. "We have something to tell you, Princess."

He glanced awkwardly at Georgia.

Natasha felt a measure of relief. They were probably going on one of their extended trips, or maybe they had decided to buy something ridiculously extravagant. Perhaps they really were planning her sixteenth birthday later in the year. They hadn't suspected anything about her secret after all. How could they when they were so wrapped up in their own lives?

Georgia cleared her throat and resumed leadership status in the conversation. "You know we both love you dearly, Natasha, and we always will. You do know that, don't you?"

Love? Something was wrong. Natasha felt numb and braced herself. Her mother's dainty hand was covering her own, but she couldn't feel a thing. She stared at the two hands—two generations of Smithson-Blair women who were completely out of touch with one another. She couldn't remember the last time her mother had actually made physical contact with her.

"There are going to be some changes, darling. It'll be better for the three of us, you'll see," her mother said smoothly.

"Good grief, woman." Natasha's father stiffened and leaned forward.

Natasha snapped to attention at the sound of her father's raised voice. This was a first.

"Tasha, what your mother is trying to say..." His face crumpled. He hung his head and breathed in deeply. "Your mother and I are getting a divorce."

The grandfather clock, a family heirloom standing guard in the hall, ticked in perfect time with Natasha's pulse. She felt the blood pump in her ears, nausea filled her empty stomach, and the fine hairs on her arms stood to attention at the shocking news.

"William, how could you just come out and say it?" Georgia raged while she rose and stood directly before her husband, hands on hips. "You can't drop a bombshell like that without any explanation."

William straightened to his full six feet and pulled the sleek glasses from his face. "You think I enjoyed saying those words, Georgia? You want to give the explanation a shot? There's no easy way to break it to your child that her family has just dissolved."

Sudden wailing consumed the room and Natasha looked at her parents to see where it was coming from. They both turned instantly toward her and quickly claimed a seat on either side of her.

"Tasha, forgive us, Princess," her dad whispered now, his strong arms holding her in a tight embrace. "We never meant to hurt you."

The horrific wailing continued.

"Your father's right, darling." Georgia stiffly stroked Natasha's hair. "We are so, so sorry. Please don't cry. You know how I *hate* to see your tears."

As if waking from a deep sleep, Natasha was suddenly conscious of her wet cheeks and recognized the source of the continuous, dreadful wailing. The chilling sound escalated from her own open mouth.

~ Two ~

The rest of the evening was a blur. Natasha couldn't even remember how she got into bed. Someone, presumably her mother, undressed her and tucked her in nice and tight.

Just like when I was a little girl...

In the morning light, Natasha replayed her parents' words and the stark reality of divorce shot through her like a bullet to the stomach.

Before last night, she couldn't remember the last time she had actually cried. She certainly would not cry again. Crying was weak and she was strong. Her mother thought crying was pathetic, so Natasha very rarely allowed herself an outburst. She would usually release her frustrations by shouting or even dancing, but never crying. Last night, all that emotion was simply a reaction to the news, but now she would pull herself together.

No more tears. Her wall was up.

Thankfully, today was Saturday and she wouldn't have to face her friends at school. The weekend would give her time to come to terms with her parents' divorce.

Divorce is such an ugly word.

Surely this couldn't be really happening to their superficially happy family? Things were strained recently, but the perfect façade was always there for outsiders to see. The feeling of being torn in two sliced through her. Would she have to choose which parent she wanted to live with?

How could they do this to me?

Natasha reached for her cell phone on the table beside her bed and leaned against the headboard. She needed to speak to the one person who would understand. The only one who would keep her mouth shut and not take delight in spreading this delicious new morsel of gossip in their social circles.

Seeing it was nearly ten o'clock, she pressed speed-dial, and closed her eyes while waiting for Bethany to answer.

Beth would know what to do, what to think. She was a bit churchy and different since her own parents' tragic accident over a year ago, but she was still Natasha's best friend.

They met in kindergarten and shared every secret imaginable over the years—except for Natasha's private, most recent one, of course. Poor Beth had been through so much, even Natasha couldn't bring herself to add to the load, until the ridiculous divorce announcement last night.

"Hey Nat, you're up early." Bethany's jovial voice broke through Natasha's wandering thoughts.

"Beth, you're never going to guess what's happened." Not one to ramble, Natasha dove straight in. "My parents are getting a divorce."

Silence prevailed from the other end of the phone.

"Beth, did you hear what I just said?"

Quiet sniffling started. "Oh Nat, I can't believe it. I'm so sorry. I had no idea things were so bad. Do you want some company? I can come right now."

Natasha quickly fought back tears of her own. "Sure. That would be good. If you're not too busy..."

"Nat, I'm never too busy for you. Surely you know that. Aunt Alice is here and I know she won't mind driving me. I'll see you soon. Bye."

The phone went dead and Natasha slumped down into her pillow. *Wow, Bethany's the strong one for a change. Maybe it's okay for me to be needy for once.*

"Knock, knock."

Natasha recoiled at the sound of her mother's voice.

"Come in," she replied blandly.

Georgia tentatively stepped into Natasha's room. Mother and daughter surveyed one another silently. Sitting up, Natasha self-consciously ran her fingers through her fine, somewhat disheveled hair and pulled the sheets over her silky short pajamas. Georgia looked stunning—from her glossy, auburn, up-do, to her skinny jeans and killer heels.

"Going somewhere, Mother?"

Georgia swayed slightly where she stood at the end of Natasha's four-poster bed. She set an empty wine glass down on the dresser and focused critically on her daughter's hair.

"Natasha, how are you feeling, darling? Do you need me to call Doctor Munroe?"

"How do you think I'm feeling, Mother? I don't need a doctor—I need a functional family," she spat. "I'm about to become a statistic, another kid with divorced parents. Like my life isn't miserable enough." Natasha turned over and buried her head under the crisp, white sheet.

"Young lady," Georgia obviously wasn't going to be sympathetic, "you have lived a charmed life thus far. Your father and I have given you everything your little heart desires—the most expensive clothes, tropical vacations, a fabulous school for the arts, with the very best opportunity to become a ballerina..."

"How do you know what I want?" Natasha yelled, throwing the covers back. Her voice suddenly dropped to a whisper and she narrowed her eyes. "You don't know me at all."

Georgia looked like someone had slapped her face. She gasped, picked up her glass, and turned to leave. Natasha watched her mother disappear through the doorway and down the hall, back into her own world of selfishness.

With a loud sigh, Natasha ignored the ache in her heart and the hunger pains cramping her stomach, and headed for the shower. There should be enough time to get ready before Bethany arrived. She didn't need to eat breakfast. She sipped from the water bottle on her table, hoping that would sustain her for a while at least.

Fifteen minutes later, she heard the elaborate chime of the front door. Maria, their housekeeper, didn't work Saturdays and she recognized the stiletto tapping of her mother's heels confidently striding to greet Bethany.

Poor Beth. Mother has been totally weird with her since the accident. Beth's parents are gone and it sucks, but I don't see why Mother has to treat my best friend like she has leprosy or something.

Natasha bit her lip while straining to hear the exchange of mindless pleasantries.

"Come on up," Natasha shouted quickly. "I'm just finishing drying my hair." She switched the drier on to its highest speed and sat in front of her mirror.

I swear I'm getting a double chin.

She observed her face from all angles and sucked in her cheeks.

Better.

"Oh, Nat." Bethany flew across the bedroom and hugged her friend tightly. "Are you okay? Your mom seemed kind of weird."

Natasha closed her eyes and savored the moment of friendship before having to discuss her new dilemma. She took a deep breath, turned the hairdryer off, set it on the dresser, and swiveled to face Bethany.

"Sorry about that—she's so awkward around you these days. I think it just reminds her of the accident. She really misses your mom."

"It's okay, I get it. They were best friends. Like you and me." Bethany sighed and sat on the edge of the bed. "Tell me everything."

Natasha blew out a shaky breath. "I know this is nothing compared to what happened to you last year, Beth. And maybe I haven't been totally great at helping you through it, but I don't know how to handle this stupid divorce stuff. What do I do?"

Tears pooled, but she forbade them to fall, and continued to rant.

"I hate my parents. I've never been good enough for them. Now they hate me and they hate each other."

Bethany held Natasha's shoulders firmly and looked straight into her eyes. "What on earth are you talking about?" She spoke softly. "Nobody hates you. I don't know what your parents' problem is, but I promise it's nothing to do with you. You need to sit down with them and chat about this, otherwise it'll get ugly."

"Everything around here is ugly," Natasha wailed. "You know how my mom is—such a perfectionist, always criticizing me, and shouting at Daddy. Why can't she love me the way I am? Am I really that ghastly?"

Bethany squashed Natasha with another warm hug. "Nat, you're the best friend I've ever had. You're stunning and brilliant and funny, and you're a born leader. After Mom and Dad's accident, you were the first friend who came to the hospital to see me, brought me my favorite brownies, and you even went to that disastrous bonfire party with me. Remember?"

Natasha nodded. "But I can be a brat. I know that. I simply can't understand why they are going through with this. I can't handle the thought of Daddy not living here anymore. I'll probably have to choose between them and then we'll have to move. What if I have to change schools? Oh my goodness—my life is a disaster."

"Calm down," Bethany said, pulling Natasha to her feet. "I don't know what you're going through exactly, but I really think communication is the most important thing between you and both of your parents. Don't you agree?"

Natasha grabbed a leather belt from a chair and thought quietly while she threaded it through the belt loops of her black skinny jeans.

"Honestly, I don't even know what the major problem can be. Nothing huge has changed around here recently, not that I've noticed anyway. It's the same false family façade as always. They've not been the same since your accident, that's for sure. Your parents were more like family to us, and I know we were all pretty low for a while." Natasha stopped fiddling with her belt and looked into her friend's huge, chocolate brown eyes. "I still can't believe they've gone."

"Me either." Bethany swiped at a tear and sighed.

"I'm kind of scared," Natasha admitted.

"Of the divorce and everything?"

"Yeah, but I think I'm scared of finding out some deep, dark secret. What if one of them has done something unforgivable?" Natasha couldn't meet Bethany's gaze.

"Look, Nat, why don't you ask them? Try to have a civil conversation and understand what's really going on. You can't go jumping to conclusions. I'm pretty sure there are no deep, dark secrets in this house."

Natasha winced. "You'd be surprised..."

"What do you mean?" Bethany looked worried.

"Oh, nothing, hey, if I go and attempt to speak with Mother about this stuff now, will you come with me? She might be less likely to storm off if you're there, too."

"Of course," Bethany replied with a smile. "Try to play nice, okay?"

The girls left the bedroom, wandered down the spiral staircase, and across the foyer to the kitchen. Georgia was sitting on a barstool with her back to them when they entered.

"Mother, can we talk?" Natasha asked, pulling her cashmere cardigan tightly around her middle.

Georgia didn't move.

Natasha walked over to the counter and saw an empty wine bottle discarded in the sink. "What's wrong? Mother, why are you drinking this much before lunch?"

"Nothing I can't handle, darling, and nothing to worry your pretty little head about. I'm going to bed." With that, Georgia Smithson-Blair almost fell from her perch on the stool. Steadying herself, the woman slowly meandered through the kitchen, and sashayed up the sweeping staircase.

The girls watched in stunned silence.

Finally Bethany whispered, "I've never seen your mother so..."

"Imperfect?" Natasha suggested and then hopped onto a barstool. She looked at Bethany's bewildered face. "That was bizarre. I wonder what Daddy's done to make her like this."

Finding a lip-gloss in her cardigan pocket, Natasha applied a quick sheen to her lips, and faced her friend.

"You don't suppose Daddy's cheating on her do you? He's always making excuses to blow her off, and spends most evenings at the office, or so he says..." Natasha felt her blood boiling when she pictured her father with another woman.

Bethany shook her head. "Wait up, Nat. Your imagination is working overtime here. Your dad? He wouldn't do anything like that—I've known your family forever, remember. If only my parents were still here, they would know what to do."

Natasha grabbed her friend's hand and gave it a squeeze.

"You're right. Not that I would completely blame him, you know. Mother treats him with zero respect, even in front of other people. Maybe he actually found someone who is soft and caring and nice to him. He's a smart, handsome, rich guy—what's not to love?"

Bethany twirled her long ringlets, deep in thought. "I still don't believe he would do that to your family. He's too upstanding. Maybe your mom is depressed and needs some time to get used to the idea of them suddenly being apart?"

Natasha snorted. "They're already apart. You know as well as I do that my parents haven't exactly been lovey-dovey with each other in years. Not like yours were. We had such different families, didn't we? And now we're both in a mess."

"Come on." Bethany pulled Natasha toward the front door. "We need some fresh air and it's starting to feel like spring out there. You can come home with me. I'll phone Aunt Alice and she can pick us up when she's finished shopping."

"If I have to, I guess," Natasha whined. "I'm actually impressed at how well you get on with Alice. I know she was more than happy to have you move in with her after the accident and all, but it still must be strange with her incessant church stuff."

"It's *my* church stuff now, Nat, and Aunt Alice is a gem. You know how important my faith is to me. I don't know how I would have survived this past year without it.

Maybe this will be the perfect day for you to actually listen to me." Bethany grinned and Natasha huffed.

The ringing telephone broke the silence and Natasha walked over to the side table and picked it up. "Smithson-Blair residence," she said, doing her best Georgia impression.

"Hey, beautiful, it's me." A deep voice with a southern accent replied—definitely not her father's.

"Who is this?" she demanded, shaking slightly.

"It's only been three nights, have you forgotten me already, Sugar?"

Natasha slammed the phone down and covered her face with her hands.

"What is it?" Bethany asked. "You look like you've seen a ghost."

Natasha collapsed onto the bottom stair. "Oh my goodness, Beth, I had it all wrong—it's not *Daddy* who's been cheating after all."

~ Three ~

Natasha pressed her forehead against the cool glass and gazed through Bethany's bedroom window into the backyard. The chilled smoothness gave a moment of relief from her pounding headache.

She noticed the plethora of spring flowers making their appearance throughout the lovingly manicured area—all Alice's handiwork. She sighed, thinking of her own magnificent, artificial-looking gardens, tended regularly by professionals. No love had been put into them whatsoever.

What on earth is my mother up to? How could she even think about cheating on Daddy? I'm ashamed I even suspected him. She's such a hypocrite—always saying how important it is to keep up appearances and put family first. How could she?

Alice picked the girls up when they called, and now Bethany was fixing some iced tea with her in the kitchen. Natasha looked down at Muffin, Bethany's fluffy little dog.

"What's up, Muffin?" she asked quietly. "You seem pretty happy in your modest digs with Beth and Alice. The three of you have got a cool thing going here, you know. Don't you miss the mansion you used to live in, boy? I can't believe how well Beth has adjusted from her old life—her rich life."

She didn't usually bond with animals, but the dog was super-cute and today Natasha needed all the love and attention she could get.

"I don't think I'm going to adjust so well to change. Do you realize my entire family has disintegrated in the past twenty-four hours?"

Muffin flopped onto the floor, looking as sad and dejected as Natasha felt.

"Nat, are you actually talking to my dog? That's a first."

Bethany entered the bedroom, handed Natasha a glass of tea, and offered her a coconut chocolate-chip cookie. It smelled divine, but Natasha shook her head. "No, thanks. And now I know I'm going crazy if I'm communicating with Muffin."

Bethany frowned. "Are you sure you don't want a cookie? They're your favorites. When was the last time you ate anything? I bet you didn't have breakfast before I arrived. I hate to sound like your mother, but you really should eat something. Want me to make some toast and fruit?"

Natasha walked over to the bed and got comfortable. "No thanks. And trust me, you sound nothing like my mother. She's so paranoid about her own diets she barely notices what I eat. Besides, I don't feel so great."

Bethany put the plate of cookies on her dresser and settled onto the bed with Muffin on her lap. "Okay, but we'll get something later for sure. It looks like you've lost weight, and you're skinny to begin with."

"Yeah, right, I need to lose at least ten pounds. Fat ballerinas simply don't make it, Beth. You know that."

Bethany looked deeper into Natasha's eyes. "What's wrong? Other than your parents, I mean. I know we haven't been super close these past few months, but I can tell when you're hiding something."

Now was not the time. Natasha was torn—part of her desperately wanted to share her secret with someone and Beth was the obvious choice. But somehow it sounded so lame and weak. She simply couldn't bring herself to confess. Not yet.

Natasha stretched out her legs on the bed and decided to deflect the attention.

"Enough about me. Wow, I don't say that very often. Let's get my mind off my own worries. How about you and Mister Dreamy? Any developments I should know about?"

Bethany blushed and took a sip of iced tea. "You know it's not like that, we're too young for anything serious. Todd and I go out with the youth group and stuff sometimes, and we chat, you know. Maybe we'll end up dating eventually, but it's just nice...for now."

Natasha wrinkled her nose. "You have the most major crush on Dreamy, that's for sure. You might as well admit it."

"Okay, I like him a lot." Bethany smiled shyly. "What about you, anyone interesting on the scene these days? Last I heard, you were madly in love with what's-his-name from science class."

"Oh, you mean Drew? No, that was so yesterday. Turns out he's a complete nerd after all. Shame, I had high hopes for that one. He's loaded."

"Nat, don't be so heartless. He's sweet and obviously smart."

"Yeah, whatever. What about young and beautiful Aunt Alice and the pastor dude? Have they set a date for the wedding yet?"

"Yes." Bethany squealed, flicking a couple of cookie crumbs from her jeans. "They just decided this week. It's going to be a New Year's Eve wedding. How utterly romantic is that? And I'm going to be a bridesmaid. I'm so happy for Aunt Alice. Steve is such an amazing guy. Even though I thought he was stealing her away from me in the beginning. What a princess I was."

Natasha raised her tea glass. "Here's to princesses." They clinked their glasses and giggled like the schoolgirls they really were.

When the laughter died down, Bethany grew serious. "You know, Nat, we used to always laugh together. Just a couple of years ago, we had everything planned out. Our parents would be best friends until they were all in retirement homes. We would both be professional ballerinas touring the world together, and eventually we would meet our Prince Charmings and live next door to one another. We would have a bunch of babies the same age and watch our families grow. Remember?"

Natasha gazed into the depths of her drink. "We had no idea your parents were going to be in that dreadful accident and that mine were going to hate each other and divorce. Our princess dreams are destroyed."

"No." Bethany wiped a stray tear from her rosy cheek. "Our dreams have changed, that's all. They've taken a different course. I believe God is in control, but I know you probably don't want to hear that right now. We can still have kids who'll be best friends. You're so good with babies. You're a real baby whisperer. It's always amazed me. And we may still be ballerinas. You can't give up on that, not with all your talent."

Natasha bit her lip. Maybe now she should share the haunting secret with her best friend—be vulnerable and real for once. Her pulse pounded and she was just about to spill her heart when Bethany's aunt knocked on the open bedroom door.

"Hey girls, I'm heading outside to do some weeding if you need me." She looked at Natasha. "Honey, are you okay? Bethany filled me in a little on what's going on at home, and I'm really sorry. Is there anything I can do?"

Natasha sighed. Aunt Alice got under her skin. She seemed so ridiculously happy and content with her simple little life. Writing for a magazine, engaged to a youth pastor, and now guardian of Bethany. Her life flowed seamlessly thanks to her full-on faith.

"Alice, you wouldn't understand. You and your God are pretty tight, so maybe you could send up an emergency SOS for those of us suffering."

Natasha noticed Bethany cringe.

Alice perched on the edge of the bed. "Natasha, I know you're hurting, but trust me when I say you're among the injured here. Think about it. I lost my own parents in a fire when I was not much older than you, and Bethany's wounds are still fresh from the accident last year. Do you really think we don't understand pain?"

Natasha felt like such a jerk. "Okay, I guess you're right and I'm sorry. I know I can be a little... um, self-absorbed, but the whole situation with Mother and Daddy just sucks."

She felt her blood boil and her voice crescendo while she ranted on.

"Why is life so unfair? Why does bad stuff have to happen to good people? Why can't God make everything right if He's so amazing? And how can you two even believe in Him after everything you've both been through?"

Silence filled the room for several seconds while Natasha's heart rate returned to normal. Bethany slid an arm around Natasha's shoulders while Alice rescued the girls' iced tea and set both glasses on the dresser.

"Natasha, honey," Alice began quietly, wrapping a thick, brown lock of hair behind her ear, "I don't have all the answers. I can't pretend to understand. I only know God *is* in control no matter how crazy life gets. He gives us free will to make our own choices, and some people choose badly, affecting everyone around them."

Natasha wriggled away from Bethany and walked over to the window. With her back to them, she whispered, "I hate my life."

"Oh, Nat," Bethany cried. "You don't mean that. Things will get better, they have to."

After several more awkward seconds of silence, Bethany sprang from the bed and twirled Natasha around, almost exploding with excitement.

"I've got it. I know exactly what you need. It'll help you forget about all your own stresses and put everything into perspective. Please say you'll come on the trip with us? I just know it'll change your life. Right, Aunt Alice?"

Alice grinned and pulled the two girls into a group hug. "Yes, of course. Why didn't I think of that?" she said with a laugh.

Bewildered and frustrated, Natasha pulled out of the hug. "What on earth are you two crazies talking about? This sounds creepy."

Bethany flounced back onto the bed, her face glowing. "We were at a meeting last night and it's all I could think about until you phoned me this morning. I'm going on the Mexico mission trip. Can you believe it? And how awesome would it be for you to come with us?"

Natasha snorted. "Why would I want to do that? Isn't it dirty and dangerous? That's not exactly my thing, Beth. Surely you know me better than that. Think of the lice and spiders." She smoothed back her long blonde hair and shuddered.

"I know you perfectly well, and trust me, you need a little dirty and dangerous in your life, and so do I. For years I've listened to Aunt Alice's stories of the orphans and villagers they help each year. You've seen the photos on her living room wall. They are *real people* living in such poverty, while we have so much. There are babies to snuggle in the orphanage, and you know how much you love babies. You can dance for them and teach the little ones how to point and pirouette. They'll adore you."

"But that's not all," Alice interjected. "We go down there thinking we'll make a difference and be such a blessing, but every single time it's *us* who are blessed by them. They're truly amazing people, who are open, friendly, and content. We learn so much from them."

Natasha felt a strange fluttering inside. Her heart seemed to beat a different rhythm and she knew her cheeks were flushed. It sounded strangely appealing for some unknown reason. She shook her head to clear her thoughts.

"I don't know. My head's in such a spin right now, I don't think I'd be much use. What sort of things do you actually do? Will I really get dirty?"

Bethany grinned and nodded, "Dirty *and* sweaty. We planned it all last night. Some of the team will work on construction, some at the orphanage, and some at the seniors' home. We'll probably rotate a bit and all pitch in with the fun stuff in the village."

"Fun stuff?" Natasha asked nervously, braiding her long hair.

"Yeah," Alice said with a laugh, "it'll be hard work some of the time, but we'll play games with the kids and take them to the beach. We may get to eat a few meals with the locals, too. That's always an adventure."

The thought of food sobered Natasha for a moment. "Oh, will I be able to bring my own food?"

Bethany frowned. "You're the daring one when it comes to eating. You love to sample the local food when we travel. I can't believe the weird stuff you've tried over the years. Why are you so worried now? Besides, when we eat together it'll be mainly our normal food."

Natasha tangled her fingers through her hair, unraveling the braid. "Umm, I'm trying to eat healthy, that's all."

Bethany didn't look convinced.

Alice stood to leave. "Natasha, you should seriously consider coming. It might be just what you need to get your head together. There is definitely room for you. I can chat with your mom about it if you like.

"We're a group of eleven, and you already know Bethany, Steve and I, and you've met Bethany's friend Sarah, and of course there's Todd." She smiled over at Bethany's blushing face. "You'll soon get to know the rest, if your parents approve, of course."

"My parents will be absolutely mortified," Natasha cried. She paused and broke into a huge smile. "So incredibly mortified. Let me think about it..."

~ Four ~

"Absolutely not, young lady," Georgia Smithson-Blair shrieked and paced the spacious kitchen. "First, you spend the night with Bethany instead of being at home with me, and now you suddenly think you can just up and join their mission trip. What's the matter with you, Natasha?"

Natasha crossed her legs and swiveled on the barstool. She took a gulp of ice-cold water and then inhaled deeply. "I don't know why you're suddenly so needy, Mother, and I don't expect you to understand. There's an awful lot I don't understand about *you* right now."

"What's that supposed to mean?" Georgia asked, her eyes darting nervously about the room.

"Forget it," Natasha muttered. "I don't think I even want to know."

"Then don't change the subject. We were talking about the trip. You can't leave me here alone for a whole week. We need to be together right now. Besides, the only Mexico you know is a five star resort we went to with Bethany's family three years ago. You're not cut out for it, darling, it's as simple as that. You're a Smithson-Blair."

"Right now, I don't think that's anything to be proud of, Mother. You haven't exactly been a good example, have you?" Natasha bit her lip quickly before it started trembling.

"Excuse me?" Georgia looked genuinely shocked. "Whatever are you talking about? Spit it out."

Natasha hesitated for a second. She focused on the glass in her hand and spoke quietly. "I know something's going on. I answered the phone yesterday and your boyfriend thought I was you..."

"What? Who are you talking about? Darling, I know your father and I are having issues at the moment, but what makes you think I have a *boyfriend*? It's preposterous." She gave a cold, fake laugh.

"He called me 'darling' and 'sugar' and said something about three nights ago with that southern drawl... Oh, how could you?" Natasha couldn't keep her voice down any longer. "Does Daddy know?"

Georgia massaged her temples and closed her eyes. Natasha listened to the grandfather clock in the hallway, punctuating every second.

"Wait." Georgia laughed. "Of course, I was at the country club on Wednesday evening with the girls. I know who you're talking about. It's Davy, the bartender from Texas. I left my wallet on the bar that night and he finally left a message on my cell. I can't believe I hadn't even noticed..."

"Oh," Natasha said. She didn't know whether to feel relieved or stupid.

"If that's how much you think of me, Natasha, surely you couldn't possibly leave the country and swan off to Mexico. Goodness knows what mischief I could end up in."

Natasha hated it when her mother mocked her.

Slamming the glass on the granite countertop, Natasha spat out, "Do what you want."

She stomped up the spiral staircase to the haven of her bedroom. She plopped on the floor, pulled her cell phone from her pocket, did fifty sit-ups as fast as she could, and then collapsed. Her stomach gurgled in protest, which she angrily ignored.

The phone erupted into a crazy tune and Natasha answered immediately.

"Well?" Bethany asked. "What did she say?"

Natasha rolled over onto her stomach and huffed. "Don't ask. She's impossible. And needy, so it seems. There is good news, though."

"Oh?"

"Creepy, southern guy is just the bartender at the country club. Mother left her wallet there. No sordid affair after all, thank goodness."

"Oh, Nat, that's such a relief. One crisis at a time would be nice. But I'm worried about Mexico. How are you going to persuade your mom to let you go? I know she can be pretty stubborn."

"Don't worry," Natasha said with a smile, "I haven't played my trump card yet. I'll call you back. *Ciao.*"

The front door slammed downstairs, echoing through the empty house. Her mother had disappeared, probably just as well. The thought of more arguing was exhausting.

With a groan, Natasha pulled herself up from the floor. Her heart plummeted at the sudden, overwhelming feeling of complete loneliness. She looked around her beautifully decorated bedroom. An array of ballet shoes displayed in a cream, highly polished cabinet beckoned her, but she was too weary. Her gigantic closet stuffed with fabulous clothes and accessories mocked the sweats she threw on.

The refection in her full-length mirror shot daggers into her self-confidence. She looked into her own pale blue eyes and noticed how empty they were. Gone was the out-going sparkle that used to light up a room in an instant. Always pale, her fair skin looked almost translucent now and her long blonde hair had lost its body and shine. She clenched her stomach muscles and turned sideways.

Still could lose a few pounds. Why do I look so, so, broken? I used to think I had it all. Now I feel nothing. But I will not *cry.*

Natasha's false confidence oozed before everyone else, but in reality she was as fragile as a delicate rose. With that thought, she sniffed back any hint of tears and glanced at the bouquet of pale pink roses on her dresser. Her father obviously sent them in an attempt to cheer her up. Like flowers made everything better.

"Oh, Daddy."

She turned her back on her silly room, pirouetted along the hall to the top of the stairs, and settled into the deep window seat. She dialed her father's work number on her phone.

Natasha loved to sit in the window seat when she was younger, especially when her parents threw lavish dinner parties. She would pretend to be a princess locked up in her tower and would listen to the chatter and sneak peeks at the guests in their beautiful dresses. Sometimes Beth would stay for a sleepover and the two pretend-princesses would curl up like kittens and fall asleep in the cozy window seat. She smiled at the memory.

An efficient female voice broke her daydream and she spoke back into the phone.

"Oh, hello, this is Natasha Smithson-Blair. Could you put me through to my father, please?" She shifted to gaze through the window to the gardens beyond.

"Tasha, is everything okay?" Her father's deep, mellow voice brought a measure of comfort and calm to her swirling thoughts. "How did you know I'd be working? It's Sunday."

"Oh, Daddy, since when does that stop you? You're the biggest workaholic I know. Anyway, where are you staying? It's too weird not having you here."

An empty pause caused Natasha to wonder if she'd been cut off. "Daddy?"

"I'm here, Tasha. I guess I'm struggling with not being at home, too. I'm staying downtown at The Regency Hotel for now. It's close to the office. But tell me how you're doing, honey."

Natasha sniffed and blew out a long breath. "Not great. Mother's being a royal pain, and there's some strange stuff going on."

"Like what?" he asked, a note of anxiety catching in his voice.

Oh, nothing much, just drinking and men, she thought. Instead she said, "She's not coping very well, that's all. And I'm the lucky one who has to deal with it. It's not fair, Daddy—"

"I'm sorry, Tasha. I know the whole thing's not fair to you. I'd be there if I could, believe me. We agreed I should move out while we all get used to the idea. When your mom's ready to talk about everything, I'm sure it'll help smooth things out between you. But in the meantime, is there anything I can do to help, honey?"

Perfect. "Actually, I think there is. I'm feeling so depressed and out of it right now, and Bethany has invited me to go on a trip with her. What do you think?"

Natasha could hear her dad drumming his pen on the desk—his usual way of concentrating. "I don't see why not. When and where?"

"It's kind of last minute, next Saturday actually. She's going with her aunt and their church group to do some mission work in Manzanillo, Mexico. She thinks it'll be good for me. I don't know why, Daddy, but I think so, too. It's only for a week. Please say I can go. Mom's really in no condition to make level-headed decisions. Besides, she won't even notice if I'm here or not..."

"Okay, okay," William gave a deep chuckle. "I can't believe my princess is going on a mission trip, but I agree, it just might be what you need. Why don't you text me Alice's phone number and I'll talk through the details with her."

"Really? Oh, Daddy, you're the best," Natasha squealed.

"Sign up and send me the bill. It's the least I can do. I miss you, Tasha. Let's connect later this week before you go and you can fill me in, okay? Let me know your schedule and I'll take you to dinner one night. And don't worry. I'll deal with your mother."

Natasha let out the breath she had been holding. "Thank you, Daddy. You know I miss you, don't you?"

"I know, Princess."

Natasha smiled.

"This princess is about to get her tiara dirty!"

~ Five ~

"I'm not fighting about it now, Mother. Charlie's waiting outside and I'm running late for school."

Natasha swigged her glass of peppermint tea and grabbed her backpack.

"You haven't heard the last of this, Natasha. How dare you go behind my back and play daddy's girl to get your own way. Your father has never been able to control you."

Natasha glanced back at the woman she barely recognized anymore.

"And that's your prerogative, right Mother? You want to control me. Too bad that's the only feeling you have towards your own daughter. I'm out of here."

She raced down the hallway and slammed the front door behind her before she could hear a response. Angry that she had forgotten a jacket, and too proud to return to the house, she stormed past the fountain and past Charlie, who was dutifully holding open the passenger door of the BMW for her.

"Bad morning, Miss Natasha?" he inquired with a wink.

"Don't ask." she mumbled and threw her backpack into the rear of the car.

Charlie closed her door and ambled over to his side. He groaned while folding himself into the seat.

"I'm getting too old for this, you know," he chuckled, turning the key.

"No way, Charlie. You're the only stability in my life right now. You can't go anywhere!" She gave him her best puppy-dog eyes. "Besides, you know you love this job. You get to drive an awesome car *and* spend time with me."

Charlie laughed. "Maybe you're right. Now what's the problem in the Smithson-Blair household this lovely Monday morning? Is there trouble in paradise?"

Natasha blew a stray hair out of her eyes and pulled her sweater cuffs down over her hands to keep warm. "Oh, Charlie, you have no idea. It's just awful. I'm sure Daddy will have to tell you sooner or later, but they say they're getting a divorce. Can you believe it?"

Idling the motor at the end of the street, Charlie turned to Natasha and she saw tears in his kind eyes.

"No," he sighed. "Oh, sweet girl, that's so sad. I truly am sorry. I've known your parents since they were teenagers. Best looking couple in San Fran, they were. Thought their love was a true fairy tale." He inhaled slowly and blew out a ragged breath while they merged into the commuting traffic. Minutes of comfortable silence filled the car until he finally asked, "Are you okay?"

Natasha gazed blankly though her window while they sped past regular people doing their regular Monday morning routine. Natasha felt far from regular, but was grateful for Charlie's genuine concern.

"No, not really. I feel like I'm in a dream. Make that a nightmare. My life just imploded and I'm not sure what comes next. Actually, I do know what comes next. I'm going on a mission trip to Mexico with Beth."

Charlie whistled through his teeth. "That's great. Absolutely wonderful. You know, my grandson has done that a few times with his school and it's an amazing opportunity. Miss Bethany is a sweetheart and I think it'll be good for her, too, after the terrible year or so she's had. When do you go?"

Natasha smirked. "Saturday."

Charlie's deep laughter filled the car and Natasha couldn't help joining in. It was such a crazy idea.

"And I'm guessing your mother isn't too keen on the plan. Am I right?"

"Spot on," Natasha replied. "Charlie, I know it looks like I'm running away, but I think I need some time to process everything. I've got an awful lot to think about. Does that make sense?"

"Perfect sense. I know you've been struggling with more than your parents lately. You know you can't hide anything from old Charlie. You're wasting away and you need to look after yourself, especially now. Okay, lecture is over until later. Here's our stop. Have a good Monday. I'll remember you in my prayers."

Natasha tried not to give a sarcastic reply. "Thanks, Charlie. I'll see you later." She grabbed her bag and confidently headed towards the school.

Facing her friends was another matter.

"Nat!" Beth jumped out of her aunt's yellow Beetle and rushed over with a concerned look on her pretty face. "Looks like I timed that perfectly. I really wanted to walk in with you. How are you feeling today?"

Natasha accepted the sympathetic hug and flung her leather backpack over her shoulder.

"Like death," she moaned. "I hate Monday mornings at the best of times, but my fight with Mother didn't really help matters. I'll be glad to get away to Mexico."

"Oh," Bethany replied, "this doesn't sound good. Didn't Charlie make you feel any better? He normally does the trick."

They waved at the group of girls congregating by the entrance and slowed their steps to delay the inevitable.

"I told him about the divorce. I felt kind of bad spilling to him, but someone was going to have to let him know. He was pretty broken up about it. Poor old Charlie."

Natasha turned back to see if the car had disappeared down the road, and it had.

"I have a feeling Charlie was the easy one to tell. Our friends are going to be something else. I've been dreading today. You know how the girls are about any scandal. They're going to love this."

Bethany linked arms with Natasha. "It's okay, I've got your back. You know that, right?"

Natasha attempted a feeble smile and straightened her sweater.

"Thanks. I feel sick at the thought of everyone knowing what's going on with my parents. Especially since it seems *I* don't even know anything. Oh well, here goes..."

The group of girls surrounded Natasha and Bethany, all gushing and fake-hugging in the hope of finding out more gossip.

"Natasha, I can't believe the news about your mom and dad," Samantha cooed.

"Daddy found out at the country club. It's absolutely devastating," Sabrina said, nodding.

"Who will you live with, Nat?" Belinda asked, a concerned look wrinkling her entire face.

The questions kept coming and for once Natasha had nothing to say. Ironic really, seeing as how she was usually the instigator of such charades. She normally jumped on any piece of spicy news like a vulture and secretly took delight in seeing some of the other girls squirm. Now it was her turn and she felt weak, humiliated, and sick.

"That's enough, girls." Bethany put an arm around Natasha's shoulder and guided her into the school building. "She's had a rough weekend and you're not exactly helping. Could you please give her some space?"

"Thanks, Beth," Natasha whispered when they were safely in the hallway, heading to their lockers. "I don't know what's wrong with me. I've never felt intimidated by them before. They're supposed to be our good friends. My head just started spinning."

Bethany dumped her backpack on the floor and began loading textbooks into her locker. "I know you're the one who always has it together, Nat, but I think this time you need me to look out for you." She smiled at Natasha and shrugged. "Who would have thought it? Anyway, you need to ignore their snippy remarks, concentrate on getting through the week until Spring Break, and *please* eat something. You're shaking like a leaf."

Natasha leaned against her locker, suddenly exhausted. "I know. I'll eat at lunch. I'll need something to get me though Miss Pemberton's ballet class. Right now, we should get to math pretty quick. Coming?"

"Sure."

They timed it so that everyone was seated quietly at their desks when they arrived for math and there was no opportunity for the hundred-and-one questions from well-meaning friends. Recess and lunch break were not quite as easy. Natasha spent much of the time reassuring her girlfriends that she was okay, and that it was no big deal, always under the watchful eye of Bethany.

That afternoon, once they were all changed and warming up in Miss Pemberton's ballet class, Bethany voiced her concerns one more time.

"Seriously, you are not going to survive on a few celery sticks and a spoonful of hummus. What are you thinking?"

Natasha sighed and gracefully popped her foot on top of the barre and rested her forehead on her knee.

"Let it go, Beth. I'm fine."

Bethany scowled, but the music started up and class was underway.

Probably the most grueling of the week, this ballet class always stretched Natasha to her limits. The teacher knew how to get the very best from her girls and had mentioned several times how much potential Natasha had for a glittering future in the world of ballet.

Several minutes in, Natasha caught her breath at the mirrored wall while Bethany took her turn dancing the latest routine they had been taught. She marveled at the progress Beth had made in the past year since the dreadful accident. There had always been a friendly rivalry between them for top dancer in the class, but Natasha had cheered Bethany every step of the way back, and now nobody would ever suspect poor Beth's leg had once been so badly shattered.

Natasha bent forward over her knees for a moment, trying to picture Landon and Anita St. Clair, Bethany's parents, who had been like family. It was getting harder to remember their faces and their voices. How on earth was Bethany dealing with the tragic loss? The thought of divorce was bad enough. Tears filled her eyes, but Natasha held them back. No tears. Just memories of their two families, happy and healthy, and together.

"Oh, Natasha! Someone call the nurse."

Muddy sounds, shrieking, and then quiet and still. A sensation of beautiful rest and deep contentment filled Natasha's senses, followed by cool liquid on her lips. Her limbs were so very heavy, but someone was lifting her.

"Nat, Nat. Can you hear me? It's me, Beth. Oh, please wake up."

Natasha desperately wanted to stay in the warmth of the darkness, but she slowly opened her eyes and her sweet friend's face came into focus.

"Beth, your crazy ringlets have escaped your headband," she muttered. The rest of the room slowly materialized and she was lying on the daybed in the nurse's room. "What happened?"

Nurse Penny, who also doubled as the school librarian, blew a shock of red curls from her eyes and placed a cool cloth on Natasha's forehead.

"You had us all worried there for a minute," she said with a shaky smile. "You collapsed in class. Luckily, you didn't bang your head and the girls think your arm took the brunt of the fall. How does it feel? Can you move it?"

Natasha slowly sat up and stretched every muscle out one at a time, taking care with her left arm.

"It's completely fine. I'll probably just have a delightful bruise. Nothing's broken. How on earth did I get here?"

Bethany took her friend's hand. "The janitor carried you. You were murmuring some weird stuff, Nat. One minute you were at the mirror with the others, the next thing, you're flat on the floor."

Nurse Penny gently pulled Bethany to the side and moved back in to examine Natasha's arm. "So, young lady, have you been eating enough lately? You know how this works. You can't expect your body to cope with rigorous exercise if you're not putting enough fuel into it. What have you eaten today?"

Natasha faced the sterile, white wall and huffed. "I'm not feeling very good today, that's all. I'm dealing with some family issues. I simply can't stomach food right now, okay?"

The nurse put a hand on her hefty hip and glared at Natasha. "Don't give me the attitude, Miss Smithson-Blair. It's my job to be downright nosy, and make sure you are healthy. I've phoned your mother and she's on her way to collect you. Fortunately, you don't have a concussion and I think this was a case of not eating enough. I'll let your mother deal with that, but meanwhile, have this juice box while you're waiting. Bethany, do you mind sitting in here while I go and meet Mrs. Smithson-Blair when she arrives?"

"No problem," Bethany replied, stabbing the juice box with a straw. "Here you go, Nat. Drink up."

Nurse Penny bustled out of the room, leaving the girls alone.

"This day couldn't possibly get any worse," Natasha said, trying not to gag while she sipped. "Mother is going to be thrilled to come and pick me up. I've probably ruined her manicure appointment or something. Sorry you have to wait in here, Beth. I guess I wasn't up to dancing today."

"Lay back down," Bethany said softly. "Close your eyes for a bit and rest. They'll be a while yet."

"Up you get, Miss Natasha."

"Charlie? I must have dropped off to sleep. What are you doing here? Where's Mother?"

Natasha took Charlie's hand and swung her legs over the side of the bed.

"It's okay, Miss, I've talked with the nurse and your mother spoke with her on the phone again. She wasn't able to pick you up, so here I am. No bother, it's just a bit earlier than usual. Bethany put all your things in your backpack, so we can get you home right away."

"I'll call you tonight," Bethany said softly from the doorway. "Feel better, okay?"

"Sure, Beth. But Charlie, where *is* Mother?"

"Waiting for you at home. Let's get you back there, shall we? Nice and slowly, that's a good girl."

Natasha shook the sleepiness from her bewildered head and followed Charlie through the school entrance. On the way home, she napped again in the car and thanked

Charlie when he opened the front door of the house and set her things inside.

"You're the best, Charlie. I'll be fine tomorrow. I'll see you then."

"Okay, miss. You rest up, and let me know if you need to take a day at home."

Natasha waved him off at the door, turned and called, "Mother, where are you?"

"Natasha, darling." Georgia's voice echoed through the house from the kitchen, followed closely by her stilettos punctuating her every step on the tiles. "Come and sit. Come and sit," she fussed.

Natasha followed her into the living room and flopped onto one of the leather couches. She observed her mother, who was clutching her half-empty wine glass to her chest looking incredibly awkward.

"Mother, are you drinking in the middle of the afternoon?"

Georgia's sympathetic face hardened. "That is none of your business. More to the point, your nurse suspects you haven't been eating properly—what's with that?"

Ignoring the question, Natasha pulled her feet up onto the couch and laid her head back. "That's why Charlie picked me up—you're drunk. I can't believe it. Guess this divorce thing is really getting to you. But you have a nerve trying to lecture me..."

Georgia stormed over to the couch and pointed a perfectly manicured finger close to Natasha's face.

"Maria is fixing you some soup in the kitchen. I suggest you start eating if you want to be well enough to go on this little trip of yours. I'm giving you some leeway with your attitude because of the mess our family has found itself in. But don't think for one minute you can get attention by starving yourself to death. I'm going to phone your father."

Natasha watched in stunned silence as her mother marched from the room, her auburn hair flowing behind her.

"It's not for attention," she whispered to the beautiful, stark, empty room, "it's because of hate. I hate you, Mother, almost as much as I hate myself."

~ Six ~

"Oh Beth, I can't wait to get out of this place." Natasha moaned into her phone later that evening. "She's an absolute witch and I can barely stand to be in the same house with her. She couldn't even be bothered to come and see me when I fainted at school. What kind of a mother is she? I'll tell you what kind she is. That woman is the self-absorbed, vain, evil, hateful kind!"

Bethany sighed. "I'm sorry to pull this one on you again, Nat, but at least you have a mother, even if she does have issues. I'm sure it's the divorce stuff making you all crazy. Did you speak to your dad?"

Natasha stretched out on her queen-sized bed and sighed. "Yeah, Daddy understands. He knows what she's like. Too bad he's not around to actually try to help. Oh well, he's taking me out for dinner tomorrow night, so we can chat more then. He seems pretty excited about my trip, which is more than I can say for you-know-who."

"Listen, I have some science to finish before the morning, so I gotta go. Please don't be too hard on yourself, or anyone else. And don't forget to have a decent breakfast tomorrow, okay?"

Natasha looked down at the empty soup bowl and proudly patted her perfectly flat stomach. "Okay. If it means I can go to Mexico on Saturday, I'll do anything. *Ciao.*"

The next three days dragged horribly. Determined to not repeat her fainting episode, but mindful of the fitted summer clothes she would be wearing on her trip, Natasha ate the bare minimum to get by.

She usually enjoyed school. The girls hung on her every word and she excelled in all her classes. But this week she was merely in survival mode, dodging the interrogations from everyone about her private life.

At home, she managed to avoid her mother most of the time, which wasn't that unusual. Charlie gave her a daily pep talk and shared in her excitement about Mexico. Her dad was trying his best to be upbeat about everything, but Natasha could tell he was desperately sad. There were dark rings under his eyes and his usual confident, athletic stance seemed weighed down with an invisible heaviness. Everyone was miserable with the looming divorce proceedings and nothing made sense anymore.

Natasha daydreamed her life was perfect again. There, in her perfect world, her body was flawless, her friends were in awe of her, just like they used to be, and her parents were back together. At night, she dreamed of Mexico, imagining what special revelation might be awaiting her. With that came her one giant fear—flying.

Finally, after a painfully long week, Spring Break was upon them. Friday's classes finished, everyone headed off for their family vacations, and Bethany agreed to help with the Mexico packing, which was not Natasha's forte.

"You have *got* to be kidding me." Bethany stood in the middle of Natasha's bedroom, hands on her head, surveying the mountain of clothes before her. "You know we have to fit everything in just one suitcase, right? The rest of the baggage allowance is for orphanage supplies. What are you thinking?"

Natasha flopped onto the bed. She was utterly exhausted. The emotionally draining week was catching up with her, and the thought of whittling down her things to fit in one case was simply too much.

"That's why you're here, Beth. Choose what you think I'll need and throw the rest in a pile by my closet. Maria will tidy it up while I'm away."

Bethany glared and raised her eyebrows. "Isn't Maria from Mexico somewhere?"

Natasha glanced to the side. "Hmm, yes, somewhere I guess. I honestly never thought to ask her." She smiled sweetly. "Please, Beth, do this for me? I need your help, you know I'm not cut out for this."

Huffing profusely, Bethany started picking up each article of clothing for inspection.

"Really, Nat? You are going to take sequined hot pants on a mission trip?"

Natasha closed her eyes. "Fine, they can stay."

"And I honestly can't imagine you teetering on the gravel in three-inch heels. And your faux-fur jacket? Really? It's Mexico—you know, like *hot*."

"Okay, okay." Natasha sat up and reached for her nail polish. "You can choose what I take, and I'll work on my nails. I was thinking neutral—maybe 'pink petal'?"

Bethany stared incredulously. "You know I love you like a sister, but sometimes I despair. Forget the nail polish, hold your arms out, and I'll give you the return pile for your closet."

"Whatever," Natasha said with a pout.

Thirty minutes later, the girls were miraculously packed. The case was absolutely stuffed and Bethany's aunt was on her way to pick them up. They decided on a sleepover at Alice's because their first flight was ridiculously early the next morning.

"Did you text your dad and tell him we're leaving?" Bethany asked.

"Yeah, he'll be here any minute. I hate that he's not living here anymore. It's too weird. I wish we could run off right now and avoid the goodbyes altogether. Especially with *her*." Natasha shoved a bright yellow silk scarf into the front pocket of her case.

"Nat, you have to face your mom. She does love you. She's just a mess right now. Please don't leave on bad terms. It won't help anyone."

"Who made you the expert?" Natasha quipped, pulling extra hard on the case zipper.

"I'm no expert, but all I know is I miss my parents more than anything in the world. You don't realize how precious something is until you lose it. Please don't throw your relationship away." Bethany's eyes pooled.

"Fine."

The doorbell chimed and the girls squealed. They quickly gathered Natasha's case, over-sized purse, and black leather jacket for the journey, and wrestled everything to the top of the stairs.

Below them, Natasha's mother answered the door to her husband.

"Georgia," he said formally, "I thought I should ring the doorbell to announce my arrival in my own home."

"How civil, William," Georgia quipped.

He walked past her and headed straight for the staircase. "Hey girls, is this case ready to go?"

"Hi, Daddy," Natasha said cheerily. "Yes, you can take it down, but watch out, it's super heavy!"

William groaned when he lifted it. "Wow, Princess, you certainly don't travel light."

"I'll find a real man to carry it down if you're having difficulties, William," Georgia said with a snarl.

"Mother," Natasha snapped. "Can't you be nice for one minute?"

Georgia feigned a look of indignation and gasped. "I was only trying to help. I'm thinking of your father's back. He's not getting any younger, you know."

William dumped the case in the entrance hall and stood toe to toe with his wife.

"Unlike you, at least I'm embracing growing older gracefully and refuse to have any surgery to suggest otherwise."

The crack came out of nowhere.

Natasha yelped and grabbed Bethany's hand where they stood at the bottom of the stairs. Georgia had simultaneously thrown her wineglass at the wall and slapped William squarely on the cheek—hard.

Natasha's stomach churned and she covered her mouth for fear she would throw up right there on the stairs. Occasional caustic remarks and cutting sarcasm between her parents were common, but she had never witnessed such a physical outburst. The looming divorce choked her and she started wondering if other fighting had gone on without her knowledge. Clearly, she had been living with her head in the clouds when a storm was brewing right in front of her.

Bethany squeezed Natasha's hand and whispered, "This is awkward."

The moment of silence was broken by another chime of the doorbell.

Natasha threw her head back, put her nose in the air, and turned to Bethany, who looked thoroughly mortified by the whole scenario.

"Come on, Beth, our ride is here and I need to get away from this."

William and Georgia were frozen in place until Natasha stormed past them and whispered, "Pull yourselves together."

She opened the door, and hoped the burst of fresh air would diffuse some of the tension in the hall. Alice was all smiles and grace, as usual.

"Hi everyone, are we ready to go?" she asked.

"Um-m, yes I think so," Bethany mumbled. Grabbing her jacket and purse from the closet she hurried to the door.

Natasha rushed over to her father and gave him a long hug.

"Sorry about that. I love you, Princess," he whispered.

"Love you, too, Daddy," she replied with one last squeeze.

Alice handed Georgia a slip of paper. "Georgia, here's the phone number of the villa where we're staying. We'll be out most days, but you might catch us in the late evening. Please don't worry, I'll make sure Natasha is safe and sound at all times. This will be such an amazing experience for her."

Natasha glanced at her mother. She looked distant. It was hard to say whether she was sad or angry, but either way, they should get out quickly.

"Goodbye, Mother." Natasha leaned in for an awkward hug. "I'll see you in a week."

"Goodbye, Natasha. Be careful."

And that was that. Goodbyes were over and in true Smithson-Blair style, not a single tear was shed.

~ Seven ~

After the drama of Friday night, Saturday morning couldn't come quickly enough for Natasha. She needed distance from her mother and her parents needed time to work things out amicably. But she was about to begin flight number two and was having second thoughts. Nothing much scared Natasha, but flying was her one paralyzing fear and she braced herself for the second take-off of the day.

What am I doing here? We're not even flying first class.

Closing her eyes, Natasha took several deep breaths to keep the growing nausea at bay. Taking off and landing were the worst, although the actual flying wasn't much better. Thankfully, Bethany sat next to her in cattle class and they had flown together many times over the years. She felt hot and sticky in her leather jacket, but dared not move.

Let's get this thing up in the air...

"You okay, Nat? You look kind of pale," Bethany whispered discreetly. "I told you to eat a bagel at breakfast. It would have helped for sure."

"I'm fine. At least I will be, once we're up. You know how I detest flying. Am I squeezing your arm too tightly? Oh, here we go..."

Natasha's empty stomach flipped when the force hit and the plane picked up speed. She squeezed her eyes shut, trying not to draw blood from Bethany's wrist. The crazy free-fall sensation took over and they were up. She let out the breath she'd held for way too long. Dark spots swam before her eyes. Maybe she should have eaten a little something after all.

"Can I have my arm back now?" Bethany asked with a sympathetic smile.

"Oh, yeah, sorry about that. Thank goodness it was you sitting next to me and not some poor unsuspecting stranger." Natasha released her friend's hand and bent over to reach inside her purse, ignoring the light-headedness. She grabbed a small bag of almonds from the side pocket and pulled them open.

"I would have thought you'd be eating a little more sensibly since you scared me half to death on Monday, Nat. Do you want something a bit more filling? I've got a stash of goodies in my backpack."

Natasha popped an almond in her mouth and chewed slowly.

"I'm being proactive, that's all. Goodness knows what unhealthy Mexican food we'll be fed this next week. I have to fit into my jeans on the way home you know."

Natasha sensed her friend staring at her.

"What now?"

"Nothing. I'm worried about you, that's all. You look different somehow. And I don't think it's just the stress of the past week. You can't hide it from me."

"You wouldn't understand."

"Seriously?" Beth swiveled beneath her seatbelt to face Natasha. "Remember what a mess I was after Mom and Dad died? I hated everything and everybody, myself included. I was an inch away from ending it all with a stupid bottle of pills. Any feelings of self-loathing you might have, I've been there, trust me."

"Is everything all right?" A male voice came from the seat behind them.

Bethany's face turned scarlet and she turned towards the aisle. "Sorry, Steve, we were just... talking. I didn't realize I was being so loud."

"Hey, no problem." Steve chuckled. "Better to hash it out before the hard work begins. We've all got to get along for a full week."

Natasha wagged her finger in Bethany's face. "Now you've upset the Youth Pastor, your future uncle. Tsk, tsk."

Bethany flopped in her seat, clearly defeated. "Whatever."

In the silence, Natasha occupied her mind by thinking about her traveling companions.

She already knew five of them. There was Bethany, Aunt Alice, Pastor Steve, and then there was "Dreamy" Todd, and shy Sara with the turquoise eyes. She was kind of quiet and plain, but Beth seemed to think she was wonderful.

There were also the new people she met this morning for the first time when everyone hopped on the church bus, six of them altogether. A young married couple, Peter and Caron, way too young to be married in Natasha's opinion. And there was Chelsea and Harmony, two girls in their first year at University who seemed friendly enough, plus two boring guys in their twenties. Natasha was too tired to remember their names—so incredibly tired.

"Nat, wake up. We're here and you're drooling in your sleep. Look out the window. The runway is on the beach."

Horrified, Natasha quickly swiped at her chin and realized some of her almonds had fallen onto her lap. She stuffed them back in the bag, popping one in her mouth. "I can't believe I slept the whole time. I must have really been tired. I didn't read any of my magazines." She stretched as much as possible in the cramped area and peered through the rounded window. "Oh no, here we go again..."

This time Bethany grabbed her hand and gave it a comforting squeeze. "Don't worry, I'll pray you down." She waggled her eyebrows and grinned before closing her eyes.

Natasha held her breath for the descent and before she knew it, the plane landed smoothly with the gentlest of jolts. "Whew, we made it. I guess your prayers worked. But why do I have a feeling the flight was the easy part of this trip?"

Bethany flashed a smile and gathered her belongings. "I think it's going to be the most life-changing experience ever."

Natasha frowned. "And that's exactly what I'm worried about."

~ * ~

On the journey from the airport to the town, the excited San Francisco mission team fully embraced Natasha and she had a feeling Bethany had primed them on her princess-like quirks. They were an easy-going bunch and went out of their way to be nice to her. The guys reassured her that the dead tarantula on the road was nothing to be afraid of, and Steve gave her some practical advice about scorpions and other safety measures she should heed.

Even so, she couldn't help feeling like an outsider, the only "un-churchy" one there. She observed her traveling companions critically and sighed.

This has the potential of being the most awkward week of my entire life.

When they eventually arrived at their villa, Natasha was relieved beyond words. It didn't seem too horrendous at all. In fact, some would even call it charming. It certainly could have been worse.

The hot, sticky team piled out of their rickety minivan and surveyed their temporary home. Alice, Pastor Steve, and the two older guys had been here before, but this was brand new for the rest of them. Natasha pushed her bag over her shoulder and slid her oversized sunglasses from her face to get a better look. A balmy, warm breeze blew her long, straight hair across her eyes and she promptly tied it back in a ponytail.

"Not bad," she muttered. Shading her eyes, Natasha took in the whitewashed building covered with vines and bright pink flowers. "A bit old and in need of a facelift, but I think I see a pool out back. Beth, is that a pool?"

Bethany's mouth was open while she stared motionless at the villa, her crazy long, brown ringlets bouncing about her shoulders in the gentle wind. Natasha noticed one solitary tear sliding down her friend's cheek.

She gently touched Bethany's arm. "Beth, what's wrong? Don't you like it? It's really not *that* bad, and that's huge coming from me."

"No, it's not that," Bethany sniffed and brushed the tear away. "It's so beautiful. Mom and Dad would have loved it. But they'll never get to see it, and I can't even tell them about it. Sorry, I'm fine, really. It just seems like every new experience I have, I still include them. I guess it's part of the whole grieving thing."

Alice came by and gave Bethany a hug. Presumably, the aunt was used to Bethany's emotional rollercoaster. Natasha felt guilty for not being there enough for her best friend this past year. Her thoughts turned briefly to her own parents and she shivered despite the unbearable heat.

"Okay, guys," Steve yelled above the chattering. "This is it—home sweet home for the next week. Your house, *su casa*. I know you're all wiped, but we need to get unpacked and set up so that dinner can be made. I've mentioned it before—please watch out for the scorpions."

Natasha shuddered. She'd already been briefed on the dangers of the little brown poison-carriers, but she was certainly not ready to meet one.

Steve continued, "Shoes on at all times. Okay, grab your stuff, you know who you're rooming with. Let's get moving."

"I can't believe we have to share with Alice and Sara. How come those other girls from Uni get a room with just the two of them?" Natasha complained.

Bethany shrugged. "Aunt Alice thought we'd prefer the bigger room at the back. She knows her way around, so I think we need to trust her. Don't pout, Nat. Let's get out of this heat."

"I'm not pouting," Natasha argued. "I simply don't know why we couldn't stay at a nice resort."

"The castle not big enough for Princess Natasha?" Todd whispered on his way past, a huge grin on his handsome face.

"Of all the cheek," Natasha blurted out, noticing him wink at Bethany before ducking into the villa.

"He's only teasing," Bethany assured her.

"I'll show him teasing. And quit blushing, Beth—it's pathetic."

They grabbed their gear and followed the others through the huge, carved wooden doorway. Everyone was tired and hungry, and decided to dump their cases in the bedrooms and meet back at the kitchen.

"Hey, Dreamy," Natasha said when she brushed by Todd. "Your girlfriend's room is up this way."

Bethany gasped and dragged Natasha by the arm straight into their bedroom.

"Nat, I can't believe you said that." Tears pooled in Bethany's hurt eyes. "I told you we're not dating. And at this rate, he'll never want to. How could you?"

Natasha dropped her things in a pile on the tiled floor.

"I couldn't help myself. You know how I am when I'm overtired."

"Maybe you should eat something."

"Maybe you should mind your own business."

"Girls?" Alice appeared at the doorway and looked from Bethany to Natasha. "Everything okay?"

"Wow." Sara followed Alice in, and rushed over to open the French doors. "Look at this view—I've never seen anything like it."

The others joined Sara and poured out onto the private balcony. Before them was a huge expanse of sky above an ocean of the deepest blue. Palm trees covered the ground from their villa to the beach, and the entire scene took Natasha's breath away.

"Oh, Aunt Alice," Bethany squealed, "this is amazing. Thank you for choosing this room for us. No wonder you love it here so much."

Natasha was momentarily speechless. She marveled at the sight before her and knew she was in a special place. Maybe this would be a week full of miracles.

"Not too shabby," she muttered. "I think even Mother would approve of a view like this one. Maybe it's not going to be so bad after all."

~ Eight ~

"Wakey, wakey, girls!"

The sound of Alice's cheery voice made Natasha want to curl up in a ball and die. Last night at dinner, Alice fussed over everyone making sure they all had enough to eat. Didn't she realize dancers eat like pigeons? She lived with Bethany for goodness sake and Beth was certainly no glutton. Natasha *may* have overreacted when Alice piled pasta onto her plate. She cringed, remembering her little temper-tantrum followed by the smashed plate. Why did she let her emotions get the better of her? And why had she thrown the plate at a wall?

It had been totally embarrassing, and now the thought of facing everyone again made her stomach churn. And rumble.

There were assorted groans when the three girls stretched and sat up in their bunk beds. Natasha claimed the top bunk with Bethany below and opposite them, Sara slept on the top, with Alice on the bottom. Who would have guessed painfully quiet Sara would snore like a freight train? Unbelievable.

Natasha rubbed her tired eyes and then ran her fingers through her long, once silky hair. She winced when her hand came away with several strands, dead and brittle.

What am I doing to myself?

She sighed and gazed at her humble surroundings. In the morning light, the room looked spacious and airy. Its harsh, white walls felt cold and oozed basic, but Natasha had to admit, with the killer view, it was easily the nicest room in the villa, even if it meant sharing with the freight train and the overly joyful aunt.

"Breakfast is in thirty minutes and we leave for church in an hour," Alice announced happily, before disappearing in the direction of the kitchen.

"Peachy," Natasha mumbled and grabbed her sparkly, pink flip-flops from the bedpost. Alice suggested they all keep their footwear handy—bare feet was not an option with sneaky scorpions lying in wait. "I get the bathroom first," she proclaimed, carefully climbing down the ladder runs to the tiled floor.

"Don't be long, Nat," Bethany said with a yawn. "Remember we have to share between the four of us."

"Whatever..."

Natasha commandeered the bathroom for a full twenty minutes, luxuriating under the pitiful yet thankfully hot stream of water with her favorite shower gel and shampoo. That left Bethany and Sara with five minutes each to get showered and ready, but they didn't seem to mind too much. Clearly, there was only room for one princess.

The dinner bell in the kitchen announced breakfast throughout the three-story villa, and everyone congregated noisily at the large, rustic dining table. Natasha avoided eye contact with anyone.

Steve prayed over the food—they seemed to pray about everything and everyone on this trip. It was foreign to Natasha, but she was getting used to the whole praying thing, so she just went with it. She figured she might as well try to blend in. Although after praying, one quick glance at her teammates told her she may be a tad overdressed and definitely wasn't doing well in the blending in department.

"Beth," she whispered while choosing a ripe mango from the breakfast selection, "I thought we were going to church. Why don't these people dress up? I thought that was the whole point."

The girls were the first to sit at the table. "Don't worry about it. Alice and I are wearing skirts, too. I'm pretty sure God won't mind if you're in jeans or a ball gown, as long as you're there. He's more interested in your heart."

"Great," Natasha grunted.

"Fabulous dress though, Nat. Why don't you wear it with flip-flops and a messy bun if you feel a bit over the top?"

"Fine."

Alice and Steve sat opposite them and Natasha decided to take the plunge—humble pie for breakfast.

"Listen, I'm sorry about last night," she began, staring at her mango. "I lost my temper for no good reason and I was rude. I shouldn't act like such a princess, it's kind of a trait I'm afraid. I'm used to eating and doing whatever I want at home, no questions asked. I'll pay for the smashed up plate, of course. I guess I'm a bit touchy at the moment."

"Just a bit," Bethany quipped.

Natasha was about to glower at her friend, but Bethany gave her a quick hug. "I don't think I've ever heard you apologize before. Good for you."

Natasha scowled and then broke into a smile. "Thanks a lot."

"No harm done," Steve said through a mouthful of toast. "We were all tired and I know you have a lot on your mind right now. But today's a new day and I think you're going to really enjoy it."

"Church?" Natasha squawked.

Alice chuckled and held Steve's hand. "Hopefully, you'll enjoy that, too, but I think Steve means the orphanage. Sunday afternoons we spend with the kids, just playing, cuddling babies, and hanging out with them. It's my favorite part of the whole trip."

"Oh, babies. Yes, I think I can handle that," Natasha said, sipping her peppermint tea. "I actually love babies."

They don't expect perfection and they won't let you down.

~ * ~

Three long hours later, Natasha found herself stuck in a place almost as uncomfortable as church—the kitchen.

"Okay Beth, that church service was the weirdest experience of my whole life. I understand about three Spanish words and quite honestly I don't think I want to know what was going on. Were they all on something? I feel shell-shocked."

Bethany laughed and passed the lettuce to Natasha at the sink. "Yeah, I haven't seen anything quite like that before. But don't you think it was cool? Everyone was so into the worship, and lively all through the message. It was like one big party."

"Nothing like any of my parties," Natasha replied, tearing the lettuce leaves into the salad spinner. She thought of all the elaborate parties her parents threw with wealthy guests dressed to the nines, schmoozing and drinking, flirting and socializing. Then she did a mental check on how many of those couples were actually still married. Not many. Even hers were on the brink of divorce.

"I'm going to set the table," Bethany announced. "Sara, could you help Nat finish the salad, please?"

"Sure," Sara replied. "What can I do to help, Natasha?"

Natasha raised her eyebrows. "You're asking me? I didn't even know what a salad spinner was until five minutes ago. I don't do 'kitchen', if you know what I mean."

Sara smiled, her bright turquoise eyes lighting up her face. "No problem. I do 'kitchen' all the time at home. I'll chop these tomatoes and cucumbers and we should be done. It's kind of fun taking turns to do the meals, don't you think?"

Natasha looked at the girl like she'd grown horns. "Seriously? This is your idea of fun? I would prefer dancing, shopping, parties, the spa, or flirting with boys. Wouldn't you?"

"I would love to dance," Sara said sheepishly. "I'm not so sure about the other stuff."

"Nat, what have you said to make Sara blush?" Bethany asked, reaching into the cutlery drawer.

"We were talking about boys and stuff. Hey, where's your boy?" Natasha demanded. "He seems to be keeping a pretty low profile around here. Have I scared him off or something?"

Now Bethany was the color of the tomatoes. "Hush. They're in the next room planning the week. Please don't make this awkward. You promised."

"Fine. Let's get this meal over with. I'm ready for the babies."

~ * ~

After lunch, nothing could have prepared Natasha for the drive through the village. She had never seen the "real" Mexico before. En route to the orphanage, she observed pick-up trucks with beds literally overflowing with giggling kids, cardboard walls of family homes, crazy driving, bright colors, and loud music everywhere. The people felt absolutely no sense of urgency—an unexplainable mix of poverty and joy.

"Oh my," she exclaimed when they reached the orphanage.

The driver parked the mini van on the dirt road and they entered through the rusty, broken gates. Three mangy dogs lay in the hot sun, tongues lolling out the side of their mouths, flies hovering above them. The playground was ancient and run-down, a safety inspector's nightmare. The building itself looked stable and inviting, but was in desperate need of a coat of paint.

"Hola! Hola!" A chorus of high-pitched voices shouted from the building, followed by an eruption of squeals. A crowd of excited orphans swarmed through the double doors and into the yard, heading straight for the team.

Natasha felt a rush of tears surface, but quickly gained control and plastered on a smile. She grimaced at first when she realized the bundle of grubby, sticky fingers with complete lack of control was heading towards her, but the fear quickly melted. The joyful, exuberant children pulled at her heartstrings instantly with their huge, chocolate brown eyes and colorful, mismatched clothes.

Nobody ever expected Natasha to have a soft spot for little children, but for some reason, she did—especially babies. Maybe it was because she was an only child and wished a thousand times that she had a sibling. Glancing over at Bethany, Natasha wondered if she shared her thoughts. Beth's huge smile was confirmation.

"Hola!" Natasha joined in with the others and instantly regretted taking French instead of Spanish at school. The children chattered at an alarming speed and some of the other team members managed to converse surprisingly well.

Little brown fingers clutched at her hands and when Natasha knelt down, two of the little girls touched her blonde hair, which was, thankfully, tied back in a bun.

I must stop thinking about lice.

After the initial discomfort, Natasha giggled with the girls and stroked their raven-colored ponytails. The joy on their chubby faces was unlike anything Natasha had ever seen. It was so real, so genuine. She quickly thought of herself back in San Francisco with her pious friends at school—the fake friendships of convenience, the superficial happiness so dependent on their circumstances. She shuddered with shame.

Amidst the flurry of activity, Natasha spotted a blue, striped stroller parked by the entrance of the building. The others in the team were engrossed with the small children and the orphanage house parents, so Natasha walked over to see who was left in the shade. A baby was sobbing quietly—she hadn't heard the sound from the gates. With several of the girls toddling and skipping after her, she squatted in front of the rickety stroller.

He took her breath away. An adorable baby boy looked up at her with sad, gigantic eyes. His thick, inch-long, black eyelashes were wet with tears.

"Wow," she marveled. "Women would kill for those lashes, baby."

He held his pudgy arms up and before she knew it, he was snuggling against her chest. She stood and swayed gently until his sobs subsided completely.

"Baby whisperer," Bethany shouted from the swing.

"Yeah," Natasha agreed, relishing the warm cuddle.

Lola, the housemother, came up to Natasha and smiled sweetly. "You like?" she asked, pointing at the baby.

"Oh yes," Natasha replied. "I like."

At that moment, Alice appeared and started cooing over the baby.

"Is this little Ricardo?" she asked Lola.

"Si, he eighteen month now, senorita."

Natasha held him closer, and turned to Alice. "What's his story?" she asked, suddenly needing to know.

Alice picked up a darling little girl who was starting to fuss.

"Hmm, let's see. We met him last year," she began. "He was a couple of months old and I think his mom is in jail. Dad's out of the picture and the other relatives couldn't take on another mouth to feed, so he was dropped here."

Natasha was speechless. She held the chunky bundle tight and got her emotions in check.

"Looks like he's found a favorite," Alice said with a smile. "Why don't you sit on the swing with him? I don't think he wants you to put him down in a hurry."

The rest of the afternoon was surreal to Natasha. It might have been the lack of sleep or not enough food, but Natasha was completely caught up in the wonder of this orphanage. The children made her heart want to burst. She had never felt such immediate love.

She had to pinch herself when she thought of her home life and then watched these children. Most of them had been abandoned, some permanently, and others for a season until their families could afford to have them home. But these little ones seemed oblivious to the hardship and heartache they experienced. They were happy... beyond happy.

Her arms ached, but she smiled when she looked down at sleeping Ricardo. She listened to Steve talking with the house parents and overheard them say that they took every child to church each week to teach them to pray and love Jesus.

Sounds so blissfully simple.

Natasha had seen awful things on TV about orphans and poverty abroad, but here she was in the thick of it.

These children were real. They were shown a little love and given a roof over their heads—that's all they asked for, all they needed.

The team gathered around the swing set, each of them with kids on their laps, giggling and thoroughly enjoying the attention. Steve explained the importance of these sweet children knowing about their Heavenly Father and how much He loves them and cares for them.

Natasha tried to swallow the lump in her throat. Each of these orphans knew they were truly loved by God. Their joy wasn't based on their circumstances at all. These were precious, precious little children belonging to their Heavenly Father.

One in particular had captured her heart.

~ Nine ~

"I'm so confused," Natasha confided to Bethany late that night. They had dragged their sheets onto the balcony outside their bedroom, and were lying on plastic sun loungers, taking in the vast night sky above them.

"What about?" Bethany asked with a yawn. "The orphanage?"

"Yes, well, everything really." Natasha shifted on her lounger to look at her friend's face and gauge her reaction.

"Come on, Nat, spill. I know you've been hiding stuff from me. What's up? Everyone else is asleep and you can tell me anything, you know that. Is it a secret boyfriend or something?"

Natasha laughed without smiling. "Absolutely not. I've sworn off boys while I sort out the rest of my disintegrating life. Besides, they're more trouble than they're worth. I think I'll wait until boys our age finally catch up with us on the maturity scale. Which will be—"

"Never?" Bethany guessed with a giggle. "I don't blame you. I know you think I'm besotted with Todd, but we really are trying to take things slowly. He knows what I've been working my way through this past year or so with the accident and everything. Plus, we're still so young, even if I do feel a hundred years old sometimes. I think he'll be worth waiting for."

Natasha groaned when she saw how beetroot red Bethany had turned, even in the semi-darkness. "Back to me and my multitude of problems," she continued. "I don't know where to start, so I'm just going to blurt it all out. Buckle up."

Bethany reached over and gave Natasha's hand a squeeze. "It's alright, go ahead."

Natasha's voice dropped to a whisper. "Okay. I know this is going to sound super vain, but lately I hate how I look. And I mean I *really* hate myself. I'm fat and so I don't eat. Because of that, I'm moody and depressed. I've tried everything I can think of. All I want is to be a ballerina and I'll do anything to get there. Even if it means starving."

She stopped and realized how ridiculous this was sounding, but decided to keep going anyway. "That's my deep, dark secret. I know I have an eating disorder. I don't make myself throw up or anything, I just don't allow myself to eat. The smart half of me wants to deal with it and get help. I can't believe I've even allowed myself to get to this place. I know I'm wrecking my body—my skin and hair are suffering for sure, too. The stupid half of me wants to starve until I'm truly skinny."

Natasha paused again, long enough to fight back the tears she refused to shed. "Then I came down here and realized what a fool I am. I have so much—too much. Now I hate myself even more. My parents are getting a divorce and I'm a mess, Beth. I never dreamed I would become such a wreck. What do I do?"

She bit her lip to stop the tears again and noticed Bethany's face. Her beautiful friend was crying for her.

"I'm so sorry." Bethany sobbed. "I should have been there for you. I guessed you were struggling with food or your health or something. I'm not going to judge you, I only want to help. Can you tell me how this all started? You've never been overweight in your life—why do you think you need to lose weight, Nat?"

Their linked arms felt like the bond Natasha so desperately craved. She was safe talking with Bethany. Her friend wouldn't look down on her—Beth had been through too much herself.

"I don't know," she said, gazing up at the stars. "Sometimes I feel so small, you know? Like nobody *really* notices me, or loves me. Lately, Mother and Daddy are too busy fighting and pretending to the rest of the world they're totally fine. The girls at school only want me around when I'm the star of the show and that gets pretty boring after a while."

Natasha turned to her friend solemnly. "And poor, sweet Beth, you've been wrapped up in enough tragedy of your own this past year. Don't get me wrong, I'm not giving you a hard time. I know you needed to sort yourself out, and you have—I'm really proud of you for that. This past year has sucked the life out of me and it all feels out of control. My weight is something I *can* actually control, I guess. Oh, I don't know if that's the problem. I don't know what's up with me."

"Natasha, you listen to me." Bethany sat up and hugged her friend. "I can feel your ribs, you know. This eating issue is more than I know what to do with, but we need to get you some help when we're home. I know you've always been totally snobby about shrinks, but there are some really helpful counselors out there who can get you through this.

"At our school half the girls there have eating disorders. It comes with the dancing territory. But I'll come with you. Nat, I'm really scared for you. While we're here, will you promise me you'll eat enough to keep you strong and healthy? Please?"

Natasha shrugged. "Sure, I'll try my best. After my fainting drama at school, I have actually been trying harder. Maybe you could keep me accountable or something?"

"Of course." Bethany smiled. "You know I will. Do you think this is a result of your parents splitting up?"

Natasha sighed. "I can't put all the blame on them, as much as I'd like to right now. The atmosphere in my house this past year hasn't helped, that's for sure. I almost enjoyed having this stupid secret and tricking my parents and everyone into thinking I was totally fine. The girls at school think I'm on a diet and tell me how fabulous I look, and I'm not going to lie—it feels good when they think I'm skinny. I see them wishing they were me. But really they have no idea what I'm putting myself through. It's weird to think Natasha Smithson-Blair has low self-esteem, isn't it?"

Bethany wiped her eyes on her sheet. "Don't forget I've known you since we were five. I've seen you at your highest and lowest. This is nothing to be ashamed of. I know you *will* get through this. Sometimes I wonder if we go through the really tough stuff so that we can help others when they face similar circumstances."

"Like you, with your parents' accident and everything?" Natasha asked softly.

Bethany wiped another stray tear and shrugged.

Natasha thought about her own parents for a while. "I don't know what's going to happen with my family. But I guess today at the orphanage I was really impacted by their simple faith and their genuine joy, even if they don't have two pennies to their names."

Stretching from under the sheet, Natasha stood and leaned against the railings. She was silent for a few moments, gazing across the expanse of blackness.

"Beth, I felt like such a big hypocrite. Me wanting control over my weight seems so petty compared to their lack of control over their futures. I feel horrible because I have so much back home and these little orphans have nothing. And I mean nothing. I get mad when I can't decide which fabulous outfit to wear 'cause I have too much and they have to rely totally on donations. I get crazy when I put on a pound because I indulged in Belgian chocolate and they get kicked out of their families because there's not enough basic food to go around and—"

"I know what you mean." Bethany pulled the sheet up around her shoulders. "I don't understand how come I get to live in the lap of luxury—I'm certainly no better than any of those darling orphans. It's a tough one to get your head around. I know you don't have much faith yet, but I'm learning to give God all the stuff I can't process. I figure He is God after all, so we can leave it with Him. He'll direct us to help where we can, I know He will."

Natasha spun around. "What can we do to help them? I'm going to sponsor Ricardo. I already spoke with Alice and Lola about that and I know it will help a little. We have so much money, but I feel like getting Daddy to cut a check is nothing from me personally."

"I know what you mean," Bethany replied. "What are we good at, other than dancing?"

"Wait," Natasha squealed and slapped her hand over her mouth when she remembered her sleeping teammates. She plunked down on Bethany's lounger. "I've got it. Why don't we put on a spectacular ballet performance as a fund raiser back in San Francisco? If there's one thing my mom is good at, it's fund raising. And we can get our school totally into it. The other dancers always love a chance to perform. What do you think?"

Bethany grinned, rubbing her hands together. "I think you are a genius. Let's talk to Steve and Aunt Alice in the morning. Right now we should probably get some sleep. You know I love you like a sister, right?"

"Yeah, I know."

"No more secrets then. We'll work through all this stuff together. You've got so much on your mind with your parents and everything, but I'm going to be praying for you, like it or not."

"Whatever," Natasha said with a smile. She shook her hair loose from her bun and felt a little freer than she had before. Unloading on her best friend helped and knowing she could make a difference to Ricardo and the others at the orphanage gave her butterflies in her stomach.

For the first time in my life, I'm actually doing something worthwhile.

~ Ten ~

Monday morning dawned brightly, promising a day of beautiful sunshine and new adventures. Natasha woke up slowly, basking in the pale yellow light, streaming through the old French doors. She felt strangely content and became excited when she remembered her conversation with Bethany about the fund raising performance.

She unhooked her flip-flops and quickly headed to the bathroom, hoping to get in first. Glancing at the empty beds around her, she panicked.

Where is everyone? How could they just leave me here?

Natasha bypassed the bathroom and made a beeline downstairs to the kitchen instead. Everyone was dressed and eating breakfast. Some were engrossed reading their Bibles and others were captivated with a tiny scorpion captured in a jar.

"Beth?" she hissed from the arched doorway. "Come here."

Bethany wrinkled her nose and set her yogurt on the table. "Before you throw a fit, let me explain," she began. "I spoke with Aunt Alice and told her you were having a rough time and she suggested we let you sleep in just this once. Plus, you were snoring up a storm."

Natasha huffed while clawing desperately to put her hair in a ponytail. "Firstly, I *never* snore, not in my entire life. It's that shy little friend of yours. Secondly, I now have no time to get myself ready and you know I'm not good at the 'get-up an-go' thing. And thirdly, you didn't tell Alice about my eating issues, did you?" She found it hard to whisper and be furious at the same time.

Bethany ushered Natasha toward the stairs. "Of course not. That's your secret to share in your own time.

Although she'd be blind not to notice how much weight you've lost. Anyway, go and dress as quickly as you can and I'll grab some breakfast for you. We're in the village today."

Natasha stood with her hands on her hips. "What are we doing exactly?"

Beth gazed through the window and tried not smile. "Garbage pick-up. Okay, I'll see you in a bit..." She ran back to the kitchen table, leaving Natasha open-mouthed and mortified.

~ * ~

"I don't see why I can't spend the day at the orphanage," Natasha grumbled, pulling on the bright yellow work gloves. "I think that's my 'gifting', as you guys call it." She scowled when Steve chuckled. "I can't believe we have to pick up other peoples' garbage. It's disgusting."

Steve handed out black garbage bags to each team and then gave them clear instructions. "To reiterate," he concluded, "if you're worried about it, don't pick it up, watch out for needles, hold your noses if you come across diapers, and we'll meet back here in the swing park in one hour. Bless you guys."

Natasha sighed. She posed with Bethany, Sara and Alice, while Chelsea, one of the Uni girls, took a photograph to document the activity. Ministry, that's what Steve called it. Natasha thought it was more like hard labor.

"Here, Beth, you take the bag. Second thoughts, I'll hold the bag and you pick up whatever *that* is."

"Ew-w-w." Bethany faced the other way while she picked up an assortment of cigarette butts, tissues, and a tightly bundled diaper, dumping them in Natasha's open bag. "I just hope we don't find any dead animals."

Sara shrieked. "I think we just found something gross under the bench."

"It's okay," Alice laughed, "It's an old, discarded teddy bear. Must be from the orphanage at the square."

Natasha looked up. "There's another orphanage here in the village?"

"Oh yes," Alice said, shaking the contents of her bag to the bottom. "It's so sad. This area is dotted with orphanages. That's why we come back every year, to try to build relationships. We also help practically with building and cleaning, and by working alongside the people here to make the best of their situations. Our aim is to empower the people who live here to be able to physically help themselves, too."

"Not that I have any, but why don't we just send money?" Sara asked while the four of them scoured the park for litter. "The price of our plane tickets would go a long way in buying groceries and things for them."

Alice slid her sunglasses on top of her head and looked at the girls intently. "That's a really good question, Sara. This is a cheesy saying, but incredibly true of missions: 'We need your presence, not just your presents.'

"It's wonderful when people send money or gifts and they are needed, for sure. But it means so much more to the people here if we actually come in person. You know, give up our precious time and invest in their lives a little. It makes it personal. Here in Mexico, the people are so relational, it speaks volumes to come and hang out with them. Does that make sense?"

They all nodded.

Alice continued, "Natasha, Bethany told me your plan for a performance as a fund-raiser back in San Francisco, and I think it's absolutely amazing."

Natasha smiled smugly. "I don't think many in our social circles will get down here any time soon, so we might as well use their 'presents'."

"What a great idea," Sara exclaimed. "I'd love to see you two dance."

Bethany grinned. "Maybe we will get to dance this week. We packed some of our stuff, didn't we, Nat?"

"Sure did. Hey, Sara, if you like dancing so much, how come you don't take classes back home?" Natasha held the garbage bag as far as possible from her face.

"Oh, you know, not enough money for extras, like ballet classes. I guess you could say we're living from hand to mouth most months. But that's okay, I've never starved," Sara replied and laughed.

Natasha didn't quite know what to say. "Oh!" was all that came out. *And here I am trying to starve because I want to look thin.*

Her mind reeled and she was ashamed when she realized she'd never really thought about poverty in her own city, let alone her own country.

"Umm, Sara, I hope you don't mind me asking, but if you're so poor, how did you manage to afford to come down here on this trip? I know I'm being nosy but I can't help wondering—"

"That's okay," Sara said, with a brilliant smile. "I did some fundraising. I mowed lawns last summer, took a part-time job at the grocery store, that sort of thing. And a couple of wonderful people at the church donated some funds. This has been my dream for years now and I can hardly believe I'm here."

"Wow." Natasha knew she had some serious thinking to do.

When it was time for a water break, Natasha sat on a swing and looked over to the square, where one of the orphanages was situated. Three chubby toddlers were running around in circles, giggling with pure delight. Natasha's heart melted at the sight.

"Beth," she said, "I think I've been living in a bubble."

"Me, too." Bethany handed Natasha a water bottle. "I knew a little bit because of all the stories Aunt Alice used to tell me about coming down here, but it really hits you when you see it up close, doesn't it?"

Natasha took a long swig. "Oh yes, it sure does. It makes me want to help even more. I'll try to phone Mother tonight and tell her about our plan. She usually lives for this sort of thing. And I know Daddy will spread the word to his clients."

Thinking about her parents made her stomach ache. She had almost forgotten about the divorce while her heart had been occupied with other things.

"It's the least they can do."

~ * ~

Back at the villa, the kitchen hummed with activity while dinner clean-up was in progress. Todd flicked a tea towel at Natasha's legs while she twirled on the wooden barstool. She glowered at him and put one hand over the telephone.

"Can't you see I'm on the phone?" she hissed.

"Yeah," he smirked. "Conveniently getting out of doing dishes, too, I see, Princess!"

Natasha feigned indignation, although secretly she rather enjoyed being called "Princess". It reminded her of her father. He had given her the nickname at a frighteningly early age.

"Beth, can you please explain to Dreamy why my phone call is way more important than drying dishes?"

Steve grabbed the tea towel from Todd, diffusing the brewing storm.

"I'll dry, no biggie," he said. "Besides, my beautiful fiancée is washing and I'll take any excuse I can to stand next to her."

"Barf," Natasha muttered.

"Fine," Todd conceded, "have your dishes. But I still think the princess could be doing a little more to help out." He grinned at Natasha and then looked over at Bethany. "I'm going to the balcony with my guitar. Coming?"

Bethany blushed, nodded, and avoiding Natasha's disgusted expression, she followed Todd through the French doors.

"Cute," Alice said from the sink.

"Gross," Natasha replied. "They are so in denial. They'll be engaged before you know it."

Alice turned and faced Natasha, soapy suds dripping from her wet hands.

"They are a little young, don't you think?" she asked with a furrowed brow.

"My parents were only fifteen when they started dating." Natasha regretted offering information about her parents as soon as the words were out. "Not that they're the greatest example of a long lasting relationship."

"Oh, sweetheart." Alice wiped her hands on her shorts and rushed over to the breakfast bar. She hugged Natasha gently from the side, being careful not to get tangled in the phone wire. Natasha tried not to bristle. "I can't imagine how hard this must be for you. Try not to worry about them. We're praying they will still be able to work things out."

"Whatever," Natasha mumbled.

Alice wiped down the counters. "Still no answer at home?"

Natasha squirmed off the stool and set the receiver down.

"I don't know why I'm even trying to get hold of my mother after the way she's acted recently. But I really want to tell her about my fundraising idea and I have an uneasy feeling. I guess I just wanted to check up on her and make sure all is well."

"I'm sure she'll be very proud of you. The performance is a wonderful plan and maybe something like this fundraiser will bring you two closer." Alice shrugged.

"Hmm, don't hold your breath there. But it's weird. I've been trying for hours on and off. Mother is always home by this time."

"Maybe she decided to go out with friends?" Steve suggested from the sink.

"Or she could be visiting your grandma..." Alice offered.

"You don't know anything about my mother, so please don't make assumptions that she would be doing something nice like visiting my crotchety old grandma." Natasha gazed through the window to the ocean in the distance. "You don't know what she's like. I don't even know anymore. She's not herself these days. I guess none of us are. But something's not right, I can feel it."

Steve joined them at the breakfast bar.

"Why don't you go and get some fresh air with the others, Natasha?" he suggested. "And then we can try again in an hour or so."

Natasha picked up her cardigan from the back of a chair. "No. I think I'll have an early night and try again first thing tomorrow." She stopped and turned to face them. "I know you're both trying to help, but I need to work this out myself. And quite honestly, I want to be alone. I don't want to be out there listening to everyone laugh and sing to God and be jolly. I don't exactly have much to be jolly about right now, do I? I'm done with you happy people."

Natasha turned quickly and left two of the sweetest people she had ever known staring open-mouthed at her crazy mood swing while she stalked away to find solitude.

~ Eleven ~

The next morning, Natasha watched the team gradually trickle into the kitchen and was careful to avoid making eye contact with Steve and Alice. Here was another apology she would have to make. She certainly wasn't used to explaining her attitude or actions and it wasn't exactly something that came naturally.

She was determined to speak with her mother before they all headed out to the seniors' home today. Originally, she wanted to share her idea for the fundraising performance, but now she needed to shout at her mother for making her worry. While she twisted the phone cord between her fingers, she listened to the clang of cutlery and excited chatter at the table.

"So, what will we actually have to do at the seniors' home?" Sara asked Steve, who was busy wolfing down a bowl of cereal.

"Whatever they need us to do," he replied. "They have a big bulletin board outside the complex where they write the current needs such as food and household stuff. I'm thinking Alice could take Chelsea, Melody, and Todd to the store with a list."

"Really? Are you kidding me?" Todd exclaimed in despair.

Natasha couldn't help chuckling out loud.

"We'll need some extra muscle," Alice teased. "Besides, we all know how much you love shopping."

Todd grimaced.

The two older boys, Max and Reid, looked relieved. "What about us?" Reid asked with a mouthful of bread.

"Okay, here's the plan." Steve pulled out his notebook now that he had everyone's attention.

Natasha hung up the phone, disappointed again at the lack of response from back home.

"We have Alice, Chelsea, Melody and Todd on shopping duty," he continued, punching Todd's shoulder with a smile. "Then Max and Reid will come with me to the director's office and find out if they need us to help with any odd jobs or repairs."

"Like what?" Max asked.

"Like painting, fixing the fence, filling any holes in the walls. They usually get a little behind on all that sort of thing."

"What about us?" Bethany questioned, looking at Natasha and Sara.

Steve grinned. "You get the best job of all. You girls are on socializing duty."

"Oh brother, it'll be like Christmas with my crazy aunts all over again," Natasha muttered.

"You'll be great with the old folks, Bethany," Todd said with a reassuring smile. "And Sara, your awesome Spanish will come in really handy. Hmm, Princess Natasha, you could...well, you could dance for them or something."

Natasha huffed. "Listen, Dreamy, someone's got to look after the seniors while you're off on your prissy little shopping trip."

"Okay, you two, that's enough." Steve raised his voice slightly to let them know it was time to quit. "But Todd, I have to say you might actually be onto something."

"Yes," Bethany agreed. "Do you really think they would enjoy watching a mini-performance? Nat and I brought our ballet shoes in case the kids at the orphanage wanted to see some dancing. Why not brighten up the day for the seniors?"

Alice clapped in delight. "They'll absolutely love it."

Todd shook his head in disbelief. "Man, I'm good," he said with a laugh and was promptly thumped on the arm again by Steve.

"What do you think, Natasha?" Todd challenged. "Are you up for it?"

Natasha slid from the stool, twisted her long, blonde hair into a topknot, and proceeded to pirouette effortlessly through the kitchen, much to the delight of the others.

"Not much of a challenge," she replied with a triumphant smile.

"I could be the interpreter," Sara offered. "I have a feeling we're in for quite a show."

"Okay, guys," Alice called from the sink. "Everyone finish up breakfast, and let's aim to leave in fifteen minutes. We have an exciting day ahead."

A flurry of activity followed and Natasha quickly ate a mango and coconut yogurt, even though her stomach was unsettled. She was the last one sitting at the wooden table, her head in her hands until Alice joined her.

"Natasha, are you alright? You know you don't have to dance if you're not feeling up to it."

"It's not that," she said quietly. "I still can't get an answer at home and I can't shake this bad feeling I have." She pushed back from the table, her chair screeching on the tile floor. "Anyway, I refuse to let my mother ruin my time down here, so I'm going to go grab my gear."

"Okay," Alice replied, her green eyes full of compassion. "We'll make sure you have time to try her again tonight. You know, I'm sure she'd be very proud of you if she could see you today."

"Whatever," Natasha snipped and then turned back. "Sorry, Alice. Oh, and I'm really sorry I was rude to you and Steve last night. I know I shouldn't take it out on you. I don't want to think about my mother anymore. She drives me crazy even when we're apart." She looked down at her unpainted fingernails and sighed. "I might as well put my talents to some use while I'm here. I'll see you outside."

~ * ~

Natasha really did feel sick to her stomach. This time it wasn't out of worry or lack of food, it was from despair. She clutched Bethany's arm when they walked through the iron gates of the seniors' home, trying not to look horrified or disgusted.

"This is way worse than the orphanage," she whispered to Bethany.

"I know," Bethany replied, biting back a cry.

Sara stood next to Bethany, seeming equally disturbed by the sight before them. "Steve did say it was bad," Sara admitted softly. "But these poor, sweet old people deserve better than this."

Steve led the way to the facility's office and the others followed in silence. Natasha tried not to stare, but couldn't get over the feeling of hopelessness in the place. Most of the elderly folk were propped up in wheelchairs, taking in the morning sunshine. Some gazed blankly at walls and fences, a few stood with walkers, watching their visitors with confused expressions.

The building looked dilapidated from the outside. The paint peeled from every surface, causing the jolly, bright yellow walls to look tired and depressed. Overgrown weeds threatened to choke bright fuchsia flowers, and what had once been a fountain was now a green, moldy eyesore. A stale, ancient smell enveloped the whole place and Natasha tried to breathe through her mouth rather than inhale through her nose.

While Steve spoke with the manager, the girls tried to catch the attention of some of the seniors. They waved at those close by, shouting, “Hola!” in the hope of a reaction.

One sweet, grey-haired, shriveled woman in a wheelchair beckoned for Natasha to come closer. Natasha grabbed Sara and Bethany, a little nervous to approach the lady by herself.

Close up, the woman didn’t look scary at all. In fact, she looked like she had once been quite lovely. Her large, liquid-brown eyes almost disappeared when she smiled, revealing several missing teeth, but her high cheekbones and full lips hinted at her past beauty. She started speaking rapidly in Spanish, and gripped onto Natasha’s slim, white hand.

“What is she saying, Sara? Can you make it out?” Natasha asked, all the while smiling at her new elderly friend.

“Sort of,” Sara said shyly. “I think she’s asking about your hair. I’m pretty sure she called you a princess.”

“Incredible perception,” Bethany quipped.

“She wants to touch your hair,” Sara continued. “Do you want me to say something back for you?”

“Don’t worry,” Natasha whispered, suddenly captivated by the kindness in the woman’s eyes. “Here,” she said, pulling her long, blonde hair to the side. She placed the woman’s gnarly hand on the hair and smiled. “Hola, senora.”

The woman’s eyes overflowed with tears and she tenderly stroked Natasha’s hair.

“She says it’s like silk,” Sara said. “I think she likes you, Natasha. She probably doesn’t see blonde hair very often. I think this lady is really going to enjoy your dancing.”

“Yes,” Natasha said with a lump in her throat. “But the privilege will be ours today.” She looked around at the forgotten people, those without families to support and care for them, and her heart physically ached. "We have to do more to help them. We simply have to."

She hugged the dear lady and followed the others into a room where they could change. Natasha and Bethany brought their pointe ballet shoes, and on a whim, Bethany had folded a couple of small tutus in her case. Perfect. Steve had set his old boom box on a table, and the CD's were ready to go.

Natasha sat and tied the ballet shoe ribbons around her slender ankles and peered through the dirty window of their room out at their audience. Sara was smiling sweetly while helping one of the workers wheel the elderly folk into a semi-circle in the shade.

"Hey, Beth," Natasha mused, "what do you think Sara would say if we asked her to sing for our audience?"

Bethany joined her at the window in time to see Sara bend over and gently kiss the wrinkled cheek of one of the old ladies.

"I think Sara would do anything for these people," Bethany replied softly. "She's just that sort of person. She'll do anything for anybody with no thought for herself."

Natasha wrinkled her nose. "You mean the total opposite to me?"

Bethany giggled. "No, Nat, that's not what I meant." She took Natasha hands in her own and gave them a squeeze. "You have done a lot of growing up recently. I guess we all have. A year ago, you would never have dreamed of being here. Now look at you."

"Hmm," Natasha struck her best ballerina pose. "Come on, darling, let's get this show on the road before I change my mind."

The girls decided to mingle with their audience for a few minutes before the music began and Natasha took delight in showing the ladies her satin ballet shoes. Some of the elderly folk gazed vacantly past the girls, as if watching some other world. Others chattered to themselves in the fastest language she ever heard. But there was a sense of excitement from most of them. This certainly was going to be a treat.

Sara agreed to sing at the very end of the performance and once she started the CD, she passed soft candy jellies around the crowd, much to the audiences' delight.

Natasha took a deep breath, feeling the familiar butterflies in her stomach. This is what she lived for, the exhilaration of dance. A thought struck her—it really didn't matter who her audience was, whether they had paid for the finest seats in the most luxurious theater or been wheeled into the shade for a free show. This was her vocation.

"I will not let anything stop me," she whispered, "especially my lack of respect for my own body. I have to get past this. I have to embrace who I am so that I can do what I was created to do—dance. God, if you're listening, you have to help me with my eating and all my wretched issues so I can have a future in ballet. Please?"

She glanced across the makeshift stage toward Bethany and the music took over. The girls knew several routines perfectly from their many classes and though the hot sun baked their skin, causing it to glisten and their makeup to smudge, Natasha knew they had never looked more beautiful. In their tank tops and tutus, there was something pure, something raw, about performing before such a captivated crowd. They were all enraptured by the classical music and the precision of each graceful movement.

All too soon, the girls finished their selection of five intricate routines. Natasha was exhausted from the heat, overwhelmed by the looks of gratitude and joy on ancient faces, and elated by the whole experience. She curtsied alongside Bethany and noticed the rest of the team had congregated at the back and were whistling and clapping wildly. Bethany grabbed her hand and they sat down amongst the thrilled audience and chugged water from bottles while Sara walked to the front.

"That was incredible," Bethany whispered. "Thanks for being here with me, Nat. I'll never forget this performance."

Natasha took a deep swig of water and grinned. "Neither will I."

A beautiful silence, which felt like peace, filled the air and with no musical accompaniment, Sara began singing *Amazing Grace*. Natasha thought back to the first time she heard Sara sing. It was at that awful bonfire party just after Bethany's accident, when the pain of loss was still so fresh. She had forgotten how intoxicating Sara's voice was. It drew the listener in, gentle, yet powerful at the same time, with a natural musicality so pure it made Natasha's heart ache—or maybe it was the words she was singing.

She looked around at the brown, weathered faces laced with tears and wondered if they even knew what Sara was singing about. One sweet, toothless gentleman raised his gnarled hands and looked into the sky and smiled. A couple even joined in, humming the familiar tune. Another pointed to the clouds and nodded. They knew. Natasha blinked back tears of her own and gave herself a quick shake. This was getting heavy. She couldn't cry. She wouldn't.

Everyone applauded when Sara finished. *How did such a shy, unassuming girl end up with a voice like that?* Natasha had an idea.

"Beth," she whispered, "if Sara would let me do a makeover on her, she could actually go somewhere with that voice." Natasha was serious, but for some reason

Bethany shook her head and poked her in the ribs. End of conversation.

Steve was wrapping the show up in his broken Spanish and Natasha disappeared into the changing room to get out of her ballet shoes, closely followed by Bethany and Sara. They silently closed the door and then screamed as quietly as possible for three teenaged girls.

"You guys danced like magical fairies out there," Sara gushed. "It was absolutely beautiful. I can only dream of moving like that. The residents were mesmerized. We all were."

"How about you, Sara?" Bethany exclaimed, "I forget how talented you are. You know you should really look into singing as a career one day."

"Yeah," Natasha agreed while stuffing her ballet shoes in a bag. "Seriously, you could make millions with that voice. And Beth will tell you, I never give compliments unless I mean it. You could be rich."

Sara blushed and her turquoise eyes glistened.

"Thanks, both of you," she said softly. "But honestly, I only want to sing for the Lord. I know that probably sounds lame, but He's given me this voice and I just want to glorify him."

Natasha huffed.

Bethany slid her flip-flops back on and gave Sara a hug.

"You're special and don't you forget it. Maybe one day you'll be a Christian recording artist."

Sara grinned. "Now that would be cool."

Natasha brushed her hair and packed up the bobby pins.

"Does that mean you Christians can only do stuff for God? Beth, don't you want to be a pro ballerina one day?"

"Oh, I want to dance forever," Bethany replied. "I have no idea where or who with, but I pray about every decision I make, that's for sure. Steve says you have a ministry whatever your job is. You live out your Christian life wherever God wants you to be. Could be on the mission field, could be as an accountant downtown."

"Eww." Natasha made a disgusted face. "I simply don't know how Daddy does it being stuffed in an office day in and day out. Set me free on the dance floor any day."

They picked up their bags and opened the door. Evidently, the day's excitement was almost too much for the patients. Some were already dozing, while others looked ready for their siesta and were being wheeled back to their rooms. The girls waved and blew kisses to their new fans, managing to run over and give a quick hug to a few of them.

Alice and the Uni girls laid out bagged lunches for everyone on tables in the shade, and Natasha was relieved to have the chance to sit and be quiet. Each of them munched lazily, lost in their own thoughts. Natasha forced down half an egg sandwich under the scrutiny of Bethany and relived the performance. Yes, she always loved dancing, but this was somehow different, and she couldn't put her finger on why.

If only she could talk to her parents about it. If only she could talk to her parents about anything at all.

~ Twelve ~

In the middle of the night, Natasha's mind was still racing and her nerves felt like they might snap at any moment. She lay on the top bunk, staring at the massive crack in the plain, white ceiling, hoping no creepy scorpions were on the prowl.

Shivering under the scratchy sheet, she listened to her stomach gurgle. It wasn't empty, that was for sure. Alice dished out the spaghetti for dinner and made sure a clean plate was returned. Although Natasha could feel her ribs easily, the uncomfortable bloated sensation washed over her and the mere thought of food repulsed her. Once she was home, she should probably see someone about that before it put her ballet future and her health in jeopardy. Crying out for God's help was one thing, but she knew taking a positive step was up to her.

Natasha worried about the orphanage, about little Ricardo, and the future of all the other little Ricardos. She desperately wanted to help. It was new, this feeling of frustrated helplessness. Life had been so easy until this past year or so, but now she was discovering different aspects of humanity, like pain and poverty. It was all heavy stuff, and half of her wanted to push it all to the side. But most of her knew she could not. It was all part of growing up.

Her mind skipped to the seniors' home. What an amazing day it had been. They stayed all afternoon, pitching in with cleaning, painting, re-stocking the dismal kitchen, and hanging out with the old folks.

She was desperate to tell her mom about the performance and about her idea for the fundraiser, but yet again, she failed to make contact. Where on earth had her mother gone? Natasha planned to phone her father's office tomorrow. She didn't want to sound needy or to make him worry, but something was wrong, and they had to get to the bottom of it. Maybe a few hours of sleep would help.

Natasha bolted upright in bed. The phone jangled in the kitchen and echoed through the villa. She grabbed her watch from the bedpost and managed to make out the time in the early morning light. Six o'clock. What bright spark was calling at this time? And how come nobody else in the room awoke? Sara snored like a bear and Alice was curled in a ball under a mound of covers. Beth was probably still fast sleep in the bunk beneath her.

She tilted her head, trying to make out what Steve's muffled voice was saying from the kitchen, and then heard footsteps approach their bedroom door followed by a knock.

"Natasha?" he called quietly.

Her heart pounded and she grabbed her flip-flops.

"I'll be right there." Natasha scurried down the wooden bunk bed ladder. "Is it my mother?" she asked quietly, opening the bedroom door and rushing down to the kitchen.

Steve kept pace with her, followed by a freshly woken, blurry-eyed Alice.

"No, it's your dad. He needs to speak with you and asked if I could hang around."

Natasha lifted the phone to her ear and nodded at Steve.

"Daddy? Is everything okay?"

"Hey Tasha, sorry to wake you so early."

"Daddy, what's going on?" she pressed. "I haven't been able to get in touch with Mother all week."

The five seconds of silence were excruciating. Finally, William inhaled and spurted out, "She's missing."

"Missing?" Natasha cried. "What do you mean? She's a grown woman. How can she be missing?"

"I know this is a shock for you and I'm so sorry to tell you all this over the phone. Is Steve still there?"

"Yes, he's right here with Alice. Please tell me everything, Daddy. What's going on? I need to know. I can handle it."

"I wish I could hug you right now, Princess." William was obviously struggling to keep his emotions in check. "I went to pick up some clothes from the house on Sunday, and she wasn't there. I tried to phone later in the day, and again on Monday. I checked back at the house that evening and Maria hadn't seen her at all. That got me really worried. I phoned Grandma and Grandpa, Aunt Sylvia, and all the friends I could think of, but no one's heard from her since Sunday morning."

"That's three days, Daddy, why didn't you tell me sooner?"

William waited a beat, and continued. "It's awkward. Lately your mother's been struggling, I know you've noticed..."

"You mean the drinking?" Natasha whispered. "Is it bad? I mean I've only really caught her this past week or so. Oh my word, do you think she's gone off on some drinking binge to drown her sorrows?"

"I don't think so, but I can't imagine where she might be," William said in a soothing voice. "I'm checking the local hospitals regularly, just in case. I'm sorry you had to find out like this, Tasha. Your mother's managed to hide her drinking for too long..."

"How long's too long?" Natasha shrieked. She suddenly realized everyone else was sleeping and waved an apology to Steve and Alice who were sitting at the kitchen table. "Is that why you left?" She whispered.

"It's part of it. Look, I've been up all night and I'm probably babbling about more than I should. I certainly don't want to have this conversation over the phone."

Natasha held her aching head up with her free hand and closed her eyes. "That's why we have Charlie, isn't it? So she doesn't ever have to drive me anywhere drunk. Oh my goodness, I can't believe I've never put it all together before. You should've told me, Daddy. I wouldn't have left her alone."

"Listen, Tasha, I don't want you blaming yourself. Quite honestly, she has been able to pretty much control the drinking until this past week or so. I guess the extra stress hasn't helped. But I think you need to be home as soon as you can. It's impossible trying to talk about all this now. We're both tired and need to sit down together and chat face to face. We have to find your mother and sort through a lot of issues. I've booked the earliest flight I could for you—it's tomorrow morning. If you pass me over to Steve, I'll give him the details."

"Yes, yes of course." Natasha sighed, torn between being with her family who needed her right now and the worthwhile work she was doing in Mexico. "Please let me know if you have any more news. Here's Steve. I love you, Daddy."

"I love you, too, Princess. I'm so sorry about all this. Try not to worry that pretty head of yours, okay? I'll pick you up at the airport tomorrow."

Steve took the phone from Natasha's tight grip and continued the conversation with William in hushed tones, scribbling down notes on a piece of paper. Natasha froze on the stool for several minutes, unable to think or move, let alone process what she had just been told.

"Here, honey." Alice snapped her from her trance by placing a steaming mug of peppermint tea on the counter.

"I'm so sorry about everything, Natasha. I caught most of what your dad was saying. I'm sure they'll find your mom soon. We'll all be praying. And you'll be home before you know it."

Natasha forced herself to respond. "I don't even know if I want to go home. Is that awful? What kind of a family do I have anymore? A disaster in a mansion. My parents hate each other and my mother's a drunk. Where does that leave me?"

Alice sat down next to her and gave her a hug. "You know, you've changed in the past year," she said thoughtfully. "Honestly, I never used to know what to say to you. You've matured a lot, but I know you're battling all sorts of terrible stuff right now."

Natasha sipped her tea, not sure what to say to this woman who had only ever shown her kindness and love, even when Natasha had been an absolute snob.

"Natasha, I don't have all the answers. I'd like to tell you an easy way to deal with all the issues you're facing. I hate watching you suffer, seeing you in so much pain. I've known you forever and you've always been such a strong personality, but I also know life has dealt you some tough blows recently, which are too much for you to handle alone."

Natasha looked into Alice's sleepy, emerald eyes. "You're going to preach at me, aren't you?" She sighed.

Alice smiled. "I want you to know you're not alone. Bethany is the best friend you could ask for, and she prays for you every single day. Steve and I are always just a phone call away if you ever want help of any kind. But your Heavenly Father is *always* there for you, waiting for you, loving you so very much."

Alice stood and kissed the top of Natasha's head. "Try and get through today, okay? If you want to stay here,

I'll make sure one of us is with you for sure. But if you're feeling up to it, we're going to the orphanage and it might help to keep your mind occupied. Plus you'll get to see that little angel of yours."

Natasha looked up and sighed. "Ricardo."

~ * ~

Plastering a fake smile on her face, Natasha joined the team when they greeted the children at the orphanage. She felt nauseous with worry over her mother and her head pounded, but one look at the excited darlings told her it was all worth it. Several of the little girls were clutching her hands and touching her pink, sparkly flip-flops in awe. She took time to tickle each child and give them a kiss.

Once the initial craziness died down, Natasha craned her neck around the crowd to look for a blue, striped stroller. Just as she expected, it was all on its own by the large front doors—only it was empty. Natasha tried to cover her disappointment while the other children clamored for her attention. Maybe he was napping or maybe his family had taken him back.

"Hey, Natasha," Alice called from the tire swing. "Lola told me Ricardo is sleeping. He'll be up soon, so don't worry."

"Oh, okay, thanks." Natasha shook off her momentary sadness and chased the girls around the sorry excuse for a playhouse.

"Oh, hello, Beth, didn't see you in there." She poked her head into the musty little house, full of cobwebs. "Whatever are you doing in here? It's totally gross."

"I know," Bethany replied, looking up at Natasha with eyes full of sorrow. "This little sweetheart, Sophia, wanted to snuggle in here." She squeezed the grubby little girl on her lap. "I didn't want to come in, but I realized this is her special place. The girls love it in here. Can you believe it?"

Natasha stood with her hands on her slender hips, surveying the scene before her. "This is the pits. We need to get the others over here and help us make it beautiful. These little girls deserve better." She almost choked at the thought of the plethora of extravagant toys she had been spoiled with as a child, especially her princess fairy castle. And she had been far less joyful than these darling orphans who had so little.

Natasha and Bethany called the guys over and gave them a brief explanation of some improvements needed on the playhouse. Steve coordinated the crew and within minutes the sad little house was stripped and tools lugged from the van over to the play area. While the guys started work on securing and beautifying the structure as much as possible, Bethany had a brilliant idea.

"We need to keep the kids away from the playhouse while the guys have tools lying around," she said excitedly. "Why don't we do a mini show for them in the orphanage house? We have our ballet shoes and stuff ready in our backpacks."

Alice clapped, Sara squealed, and before Natasha knew what was happening, she was being corralled with the kids into the building. Lola and her husband, Pedro, quickly pushed sofas and cleared toys to make space for an impromptu performance. The children seemed even more excitable confined within four walls, but while Natasha and Bethany changed, Alice, Sara and the Uni girls managed to get them all sitting down on beanbags or the floor.

When everyone was ready, Sara flicked on the ballet CD and the magic began. Every eye was lost in wonder watching the beauty of dance unfold before them. Natasha put every emotion she had been fighting all day into her moves and almost forgot they were dancing for a bunch of kids in an orphanage playroom. Dancing with Bethany was as natural as breathing and they fed off each other's energy in perfect harmony.

After several beautiful routines, Natasha and Bethany finished with elaborate curtsies and their audience broke into rapturous applause. The children were mesmerized and Sara completed the performance with a haunting song of God's love for them all.

Natasha sat on a beanbag to catch her breath, but Lola tapped her shoulder. Tears streamed down her face as she repeated, "Gracias, gracias," and she handed over a sleepy-eyed bundle.

Natasha grinned. "Ricardo," she whispered. Holding him close, they snuggled and enjoyed the song. He was still soft with sleep and promptly stuck his chubby thumb into his mouth and pressed his head heavily against Natasha's shoulder.

She noticed the Uni girls had already gone, probably to put some finishing touches on the playhouse. Todd crept in and sat next to Bethany on the floor. Natasha could almost feel the heat from poor Bethany's cheeks. *Definitely not from the dancing.*

After Sara's fabulous song, they attempted to learn several kiddie songs, ate a quick snack, and played a few more indoor games. Soon it was time for the reveal and everyone poured from the orphanage toward the play area. Natasha quickly slipped into her flip-flops and carried Ricardo to see the reaction of the little girls and was not disappointed.

Seven or eight elated princesses jumped up and down, clapping with delight at their new 'castle'. The guys did a great job fixing the little roof and even installed a tiny door. They'd fashioned a patio area at the front of the house with miniature plastic chairs so they could all play together. Someone bought a sturdy plastic tea set, which now sat on a table in the center. Instead of painting, they wove brightly colored plastic flowers everywhere, giving the house an enchanted feel.

Lola, the housemother, cried again, overjoyed at this improvement for her little girls to play in.

"Good job, everyone," Steve shouted, and cheers filled the air.

Ricardo giggled and Natasha wondered if he would ever be allowed to visit in the girls' special playhouse. She held him close, knowing all too soon she would have to say goodbye and this incredible day at the orphanage would be a mere memory.

~ * ~

Everyone was exhausted—mainly from playing with the kids and finishing up the playground project, but also from an emotional day. Natasha used every ounce of will-power she possessed to reign in her tears when she left the orphanage. Leaving Ricardo was absolutely heartbreaking, but she couldn't allow herself to cry now. The floodgates would open and she might completely drown in her tears.

This time tomorrow, she would be home and hopefully there would be news of her mother. At least she could be there for her dad. The team had been so sympathetic and kind about the whole thing during this whirlwind day. She would actually miss them all.

Dinner was finished and the Uni girls were on clean up, so Natasha, Bethany and Todd were free to hang out on the deck before bedtime.

"My mother must be the most prayed-for woman in the whole world today," Natasha mused. "I can't get over how everyone just blurts a prayer out any time of the day for her to be found."

Bethany squeezed her hand and sank into the wicker armchair. “We’re all worried, Nat, but we know God’s in control. We believe that.”

Natasha felt her cheeks burn. “Hmm. I’m not so sure He’s in control over my family at the moment. We’ve gone from being the most put-together people out there to a complete gong-show.”

Todd rested his arms on his knees and bent forward. “Do you remember when I told my life story last year at the bonfire party?” he asked softly. “I know it was a while ago, but I’m pretty sure you were there with Bethany.”

Bethany closed her eyes. “It was the most heart-wrenching thing I had ever heard. I was a complete mess after that. Remember, Nat?”

“Yeah, I know you lived on the streets for a while. You’ve had a rough life, Todd, that’s for sure.” Natasha grinned mischievously. “I also remember Beth being totally smitten by the storyteller.”

Bethany’s eyes flew open and she gasped.

Todd stifled a laugh and carried on. “Anyway, I’ve been through some harsh times. Lots of us have, actually.” He looked over at Bethany with a somber face. “But I know for a fact that God carried me through it all. He found me. Like I’m sure He’ll find your mom.”

Bethany piped up. “And He’ll find you, too Nat. You’ll find Him, I know you will.”

At that moment, Steve poked his head out through the doors. “Lights out guys, it’s been a long day. Natasha, you holding up okay?”

Natasha yawned. “Yeah, I guess. I doubt if I’ll actually sleep much, but wake me if there’s a call, won’t you?”

“Of course we will. We’re all praying—for you and your mom.”

"Yeah," Natasha said, stretching in an attempt to rid some of the stress from her body. "I know you are. And I'm actually grateful."

She turned away and whispered into the warm night, "Prayers are all I've got to hang on to right now. And I'm barely dangling by a thread."

~ Thirteen ~

It had to be a nightmare, the constant ringing, a nagging reminder of yesterday's phone call that woke her.

"Natasha, honey," Alice's voice from beside the bed pulled her from a surprisingly deep sleep. "It's your dad on the phone. I think you'd better come and speak with him."

"What? Oh, right." Natasha quickly got her bearings, grabbed her flip-flops, and almost fell down the bunk bed ladder in her haste.

"Whoa," Bethany croaked from the bunk below, "You nearly crushed me."

"It's my dad," Natasha whispered, trying not to wake Sara as well.

"I'll be right there," Bethany said, suddenly wide awake.

They trotted into the kitchen and Steve handed the phone over to Natasha.

"Daddy?"

"Tasha, they've found her. Your mother's been found and she's going to be okay."

Natasha gave a huge sigh of relief and a thumbs-up to her audience in the kitchen.

"Where was she?" she asked, desperately needing to know details.

"She's in the hospital, Tasha."

"What?" Natasha cried, collapsing onto a barstool. She vaguely registered Bethany's arm around her shoulder. "What happened? Is she sick?" Her breathing picked up pace while she waited for an answer, thoughts of Bethany's deceased parents swirled around her muddy mind.

"Your mother's in surgery right now. There was a car accident and it looks like she's got some internal injuries. Her spleen is ruptured, but the doctors are optimistic."

"Her spleen? Anything else?" Natasha asked quietly, trying to think if a spleen was critical. Alice gently squeezed her shoulder.

"She's bruised some ribs, but I think that's about all. She'll pull through, she's a strong woman. We both know that."

Another thought hit Natasha like a ton of bricks.

"What about—what about the other car? Was anyone else injured?"

"There was no other car, Tasha," William said softly. "She hit a wall."

"A wall?" Natasha ran a hand through her disheveled hair. "How on earth did that happen?"

More silence followed, enough to make Natasha wonder if the line had gone dead. Enough for her to realize her father was agonizing over telling her the truth, which she had already deciphered.

"She'd been drinking, hadn't she, Daddy?"

"Yes."

Natasha closed her eyes quickly before they shed tears of frustration and resentment.

"Why?" She yelled into the phone. "Why is she ruining our lives? And what's with the drinking? She could have killed someone."

"But she didn't, Tasha. And we've found her. Listen, we can talk more about it later today. I'll explain it to you when you get here. We'll go straight to the hospital from the airport so try and get some rest, okay?"

Natasha slumped against the wall. "Fine. I'll see you later, Daddy."

"Later, Princess. And try not to get yourself in a panic on the flight. I know how much you hate it. I'm really sorry to put you through all this."

"It's not your fault. At least she's been found. *Ciao.*"

Natasha looked at her group of friends. Bethany, Alice, and Steve were right there with her, and Sara and Todd had joined them, too.

"Sorry I woke you guys up. And I'm sorry for all the drama. It kind of follows me around," she admitted. "I'll be fine. My mother's alive and I have a flight to catch soon."

Alice scurried to the kettle. "I'll make tea for you,' she said. "The rest of you should go back and get a little more shut-eye. Another busy day today."

Steve gave Alice a quick hug on his way past and the others drifted back to bed. Bethany was the last to leave.

"You sure you don't want some company?" she asked quietly. "I'm going to miss our last couple of days together."

Natasha hugged her best friend. "No, I'm going to sit for a while. Try and get my head straight before I take off and face goodness knows what. Hey, Beth?"

"Yeah?"

"You can pray for me while I fly today, if you want."

Bethany nodded. "Every day, Nat," she promised and blew a kiss on her way back to bed.

Alice brought the mug of tea over to Natasha along with a piece of paper.

"Natasha, why don't you catch the sunrise from the balcony in your room? It has the best view and I don't think you'll want to miss it. You have time. You won't wake the girls, go ahead." She ushered Natasha in the direction of her bedroom. "And here's something for you to read while you're there." She slipped the paper and the mug into Natasha's hands.

"Oh, okay," Natasha muttered. Upstairs, she crept past the sleepy girls, opened the rickety French doors as quietly as she could, and padded over to the edge of the balcony. Her breath caught in her throat when she took in the sight before her.

It looked like an artist painted the most exquisite mural ever created. Wild streaks of vibrant tangerine, pale pink, and deep lavender filled the sky, giving way to the glowing, golden globe about to make its entry over the horizon.

The air was still and smelled sweeter than ever. She felt she was the only one on the planet, the only witness to this miracle. Part of her wanted to go wake Bethany and share the experience, but somehow she knew she was to drink this in alone.

Tearing her eyes away from the magnificence before her, Natasha leaned against the iron railing and opened the note from Alice.

"Dearest Natasha, I am certainly no poet, but I wrote this for you. Know you are loved... Alice x

SUNRISE

He loves me, He loves me not,
She let the petals fall,
The daisy could not tell her
If she was loved at all.

She studied well and aced exams
Striving hard to please,
Would anybody notice
Whether she got A's or B's?

Dancing was her heart's desire,

Consuming every day,
But even when she danced
She felt her life slip away.

Something was truly missing
A gap was in her heart,
She knew she had to fill it
But knew not where to start.

And so one summer morning
Before the sun arose,
She wandered to the seaside
To think about her woes.

She sat upon a rock and looked
At where the sea met sky,
And with her heavy heart she shouted,
"I'm so lonely—why?"

And then before her very eyes
A miracle took place,
The sky turned pink with hues of gold
That shone upon her face.

It warmed her up from head to toe
And made her want to smile,
The work of art revealed to her
Had truly been worthwhile.

And as she watched the masterpiece
Transform before her eyes,
She heard a voice – it was the One
Who makes every sunrise.

He said, 'My child, this is for you,
To show how much I care.
I heard your cries and saw your pain,
I couldn't leave you there.

Let me fill your life with joy
And purpose for each day,
Allow my love to flow through you
And chase your fears away.

And suddenly she knew for sure
This sunrise she had seen
Was a gift for her eyes only,
She knew what this would mean

She never had to doubt that she
Was loved by Someone who
Would paint each morning sunrise
Then whisper, 'I love you.'"

Silence hung in the air and Natasha willed it to last forever. She felt it here, right in this moment. God was real, He had to be. There was more to life than accumulating wealth, gaining success, and being beautiful. Coming away from her everyday distractions, her self-image issues, her broken family, her pursuit of happiness in all the wrong places, was the best thing possible.

The wetness on her face felt foreign—she so rarely shed tears. She gasped at her uncontrollable weakness. But why was crying so difficult? Why couldn't she show a little vulnerability now and then? Was her mother telling the truth when she said tears were a sign of weakness, showing others she didn't have it all together?

"What good did it do you, Mother?" she whispered bitterly. "I *need* to shed some tears, okay? Tears for Ricardo and the orphans, tears for the seniors, tears for my best friend who lost her parents, tears for my own parents who are pulling me apart, and tears for myself. I haven't got it all together and I need to cry."

Through blurry eyes, Natasha looked out again at the sunrise. It felt good, healing even, to let her eyes overflow with all her pent-up frustration, sorrow, anger and grief.

"God," she said slowly, "Is it okay to cry?"

The gentlest wind swept across her cheeks like a kiss, drying them tenderly. She smiled, her heart almost bursting within her.

"Thanks," she said quietly. "I guess You know how messed up I am, but these guys here keep telling me You love me anyway. I don't fully understand, but I really want to. I want what Beth has. I know You've changed her and I need to be changed, too. I see that now."

With fresh tears, Natasha poured out her heart to her Heavenly Father, holding nothing back. By the time she finished, she was beyond elated, but had to hurry to get her luggage together in the bedroom.

"Sorry." She whispered when her case bumped into one of the bunk beds.

"No worries," Sara yawned. "Take care, Natasha. I really hope it goes well with your mom's surgery and everything. I'll be praying."

Natasha smiled when she realized she hadn't grimaced or flinched when Sara mentioned praying for her. "Thanks, Sara."

"Come here." Bethany sat up sleepily and gave her friend a big hug. "I'll be home on Saturday, but phone me here if you need me, okay? Hey, Nat, are you actually crying?"

"Yeah, I've got tons saved up," Natasha confessed. "I've been such a jerk. I had a chat with God earlier and I think I'm going to be okay. But you can still pray for the flight."

"What?" Bethany squealed, "You prayed? You're crying? What did I miss?"

"Blame that aunt of yours." Natasha smiled. "I'm going to have a chat with her on the way to the airport. I don't fully understand, but I think I've just made the biggest decision of my life."

"Nat."

More tears flowed—tears of gladness, relief, healing, and hope as two best friends quietly rejoiced in the early morning light.

~ Fourteen ~

"Tasha! Hi, Princess."

Engulfed in her father's tight embrace, right in the middle of San Francisco airport, Natasha breathed in the familiar scent of his musky aftershave, mingled with leather from his jacket. Relieved, she hugged him back.

"Oh, I've missed you," he continued, with a crack in his voice, "but I'm sorry I interrupted your week like this. How were the flights? I know how you dread it."

Natasha smiled through blurry tears. "Daddy, it was fine. Can you believe it? This is the first time I've not been petrified on a plane. Must have been everyone praying for me."

William raised his brow, picked up her backpack, and they headed, arm-in-arm for the luggage carousel. "Oh, that's nice," he said awkwardly.

Natasha grinned and they fell into comfortable silence until they reached the carousel. "I have so much to tell you, Daddy, but first, I need to know about Mother. What's the latest?"

William pinched the bridge of his nose and leaned against a pillar, keeping one eye on the emerging cases. "She got through surgery just fine—I told you she would. I haven't been to see her yet. The surgery was late last night and I've been checking regularly by phone." He looked at the floor. "I didn't want to upset her by being there."

"Why would you upset her?" Natasha asked, her pulse suddenly racing. "You haven't done anything wrong. She's the one who drove you away and then got herself smashed up."

"Shh, Tasha, calm down." William stroked Natasha's loose, flowing hair in an attempt to soothe her. "Please don't be too hard on her. I'm as much to blame for not sticking around," he added quietly.

Natasha bit her lip and held her tongue. She had so much to spew out when it came to her mother, but something inside told her this was probably not the best time to address her concerns. She found herself sending up a quick prayer of her own, mainly for her big mouth.

"So tell me, Daddy, I need to know everything. How long has she had a drinking problem? I never suspected anything. I'm so stupid."

William put his arm around his daughter while they both watched the trail of suitcases snake around the carousel. He sighed deeply and then spoke softly.

"Honestly, Tasha, I don't even remember when it started to be a real problem. I was in denial as much as your mother. She's a master of disguise when she wants to be and does a pretty good job of putting on a fake exterior. I don't like to talk badly of her, but we both know she will do anything for appearance sake."

"No kidding," Natasha muttered. She thought of the numerous times her mother met up with friends and painted a ridiculously elaborate picture of family life in the Smithson-Blair home. "I think it rubbed off on me, too," she admitted when she realized she did the exact same thing with her own friends in school.

William squeezed her shoulder and continued. "The truth is, she always liked to drink. You know how I'm the designated driver wherever we go. I thought she had it under control, but it slowly got worse over the years, and then her breaking point was just over a year ago."

"When Beth's parents died?" Natasha guessed. "I think that's the only time I've ever seen Mother cry in public—maybe the only time ever, actually."

"Landon and Anita were our best friends," William explained, obviously trying to keep his own emotions in check. "I still can't believe they're gone. They were like family. Anyway, your mother dealt with it the only way she knew how."

"By drinking?"

"Yeah, Tasha. We tried to keep it from you and—"

"But why?" Natasha turned to face her father. "Why couldn't we work through it together? She's so—proud."

"Maybe we all are. Hey, there's your case." William lunged past Natasha and snagged her purple case. "Wow. I'd forgotten how heavy this thing is. Come on, Princess, let's grab a quick lunch on the way to the hospital. You can freshen up and we'll talk some more."

"Okay." Natasha was slightly relieved to have a little more time to compose herself before facing her mother.

~ * ~

"Chicken salad and a club sandwich," the redheaded server announced with a flourish, flashing her dazzling white smile. She placed the salad bowl before Natasha and the sandwich next to William's coffee.

"Thanks," William said for both of them.

"No problem," was the ridiculously perky reply.

Natasha sighed and picked up a fork. The subdued lighting in her father's favorite swanky lunch spot prevented her from reading his face.

"Not hungry, Daddy?" she asked when he didn't make a move for his sandwich.

"I guess not. But that's not setting a very good example for you now is it? Let's dig in. We could be at the hospital for quite a while."

Natasha pushed a few spinach leaves around her plate, but the thought of chicken made her nauseous. She rested her fork on the plate, wiped her sweaty palms on her skinny jeans, and took a deep breath.

"What's wrong? Not feeling good? Is your stomach still a bit unsettled from the flight?" William asked through a mouthful of grainy bread.

Natasha took a sip of iced water and looked into his eyes. "I have so much to talk about, Daddy, and I know you're worried about Mother and everything. So am I, but there's some stuff I have to get off my chest."

William almost dropped his food back on the plate.

"Okay," he said slowly. "This sounds serious."

"It is. I've been doing a lot of thinking in Mexico and I want to come clean with you. Our family could do with a good shot of honesty right now. So, I have to tell you. I've been having some eating issues this past year."

"Eating issues?" William's brow furrowed while he processed the information.

"Yes. I don't make myself sick or binge, but I guess I haven't really been eating enough. Well, barely at all sometimes. I've been desperate to be skinny."

"You've been starving yourself? But honey, why? There's barely anything of you in the first place."

"Don't, Daddy," Natasha interrupted, "please don't tell me I'm not fat. I know it's not logical. I've read all about it on the Internet. I don't expect you to understand, but I don't like food anymore. It makes me depressed and I feel bloated and fat."

William blew out a stream of air. "Wow. I don't know what to say. I know you had that fainting spell before your trip, but how long has this been going on?"

Natasha fiddled with her purse strap, suddenly feeling raw and open.

"Oh, I don't know. Maybe six months or so, I guess. It started pretty gradually. And soon it grew to an obsession."

"Does your mother know about it, Princess?"

Natasha felt her eyes pool. "She's too busy with her own perfect physique to even notice how I feel about mine. We don't really indulge in any deep and meaningful conversation. I guess now I realize she was dealing with her own issues."

William reached out across the table and took his daughters delicate hand.

"Tasha, I'm so sorry. I feel awful you've been handling this alone. Have you talked to any of your friends about it?"

"Beth knows now and I think Alice has figured it out. Oh, and I'm pretty sure Charlie suspects something, too."

"Charlie? As in driver Charlie?"

Natasha smiled. "What can I say? He's a good listener and he's nosy. Anyway, I've been trying really hard in Mexico to eat well and I promised Beth I'd see a counselor as soon as I can. She'll even come with me. She kind of made me see how I could be damaging my whole future in ballet with this, so I want to get better. I really do. Plus, seeing all the stuff they have to deal with in Mexico was a bit of a wakeup call for me."

"Bethany's a good friend. Let me help you find someone you can speak with. I'll do whatever I can. Man, I feel like such an idiot."

"Don't, Daddy. I think for me it was just a way of coping with stuff. I hid it pretty well. Guess I get that from Mother, hey?"

They shared a sad smile.

"So, no salad?" William asked, staring at her full plate.

"How about half? I think I can manage that," Natasha compromised.

She chewed on a pecan and then continued with her confession. "There's something else, too."

She laughed when William's eyes nearly bugged right out of his head. "It's okay, Daddy, this is good news."

"Whew," William said with an exaggerated swoon.

"I don't even know what you think about God and stuff because it's never really come up much before, but I've been thinking about it for a while. Probably since Beth moved in with her Aunt."

"Oh, yes, Alice is engaged to a pastor isn't she?"

"Steve, the youth pastor. Yeah. I couldn't stand him at first, but he's actually grown on me. Anyway, Beth and I have had some pretty heavy chats and she's changed, Daddy. Like, *really* changed."

"How do you mean?" William asked, taking a sip of coffee.

"She's confident. I know she's always been a great ballerina and we've been best friends forever, but she could have so easily crumbled after her parents' accident, and then her leg being so messed up. You remember how she nearly took an overdose?"

"I know how devastating that was for the poor girl. So she got religion then? You think that helped?" William smiled and waved the server away so they could continue their private conversation.

"Yes, well, not religion—more like 'Jesus'. This might sound bizarre, but He's made all the difference for her. Gave her peace and joy again, and a hope so she could carry on, even though it was one day at a time at first."

"So, are you telling me you got 'Jesus', too?" William asked nervously.

"Yeah, Daddy, I got Jesus." She smiled at his phrase. "Honestly, I've been in such a bad place and I thought everything would just keep spiraling downward. But God showed me He loves me, first in a sunrise and then by Alice explaining how Jesus died for me. It's wild, right?"

William leaned back in his chair. His frown slowly transformed to a grin.

"The women in my life certainly keep me on my toes," he said with a laugh.

"Oh, I can't explain it very well, but I'll show you. God's already shown me it's okay to mess up because He's a forgiving Father. And now I know it's okay to cry. I'm going to try to understand Mother and be more forgiving. Tears can be very healing you know."

"Oh, I know. I've shed plenty myself. But we should finish up here and get to the hospital. Looks like you have a lot to tell your mother."

~ * ~

Natasha shuddered when she walked through the entrance of the hospital. There were too many fresh memories of visiting Bethany after the accident. She would never forget the first time she saw her friend the day after Bethany's parents had been tragically killed. She had looked so small and fragile and broken lying in the hospital bed—and so terribly alone.

Ready for whatever awaited her, Natasha pushed the painful memories aside and focused on the task at hand—her mother. The overpowering antiseptic smell that saturated the air nearly made Natasha bring up the lunch she had forced down. How she hated hospitals.

"Here, Daddy, I'll carry the flowers."

William passed over the huge bouquet of pink roses they had picked up en route and Natasha breathed in the fragrant scent while she walked.

Much better.

After receiving directions, they rode the elevator in silence and Natasha took a moment to check her reflection in the shiny panels. She smoothed her hair around her sequined headband and pulled her jeans up to meet her silk tank top. She felt secretly joyful that her waistband was still gaping a little bit—at least she hadn't gained weight in Mexico. Frowning, she chastised herself. This was going to be a tough road ahead.

"Just down this corridor." William guided Natasha out of the elevator and through a set of double doors. They stopped outside a private room and he took a deep breath. "Ready?"

Natasha nodded and walked straight in.

The sight of her mother stopped Natasha at the door. Shiny auburn locks framed a face she barely recognized. Georgia had a deathly white pallor despite her fake tan, sunken cheeks, not a scrap of make-up, and a grotesque blue bruise staining one of her closed eyes. Her body looked tiny and frail beneath the thin hospital blanket that exposed one arm to an IV line.

William grabbed Natasha's free hand and shot her an encouraging look.

"Georgia?" he whispered.

Her eyes fluttered open, the bruised one obviously struggling. Slowly, she looked from her husband to her daughter.

"Natasha? What are you doing here? Why aren't you in Mexico?" Her voice was hoarse, a mere shadow of her usual projection.

"Daddy called me. We were worried." Natasha dumped the roses on the side table and carefully perched on the edge of the bed. "Where have you been, Mother? I thought you were…" Unable to finish her sentence, Natasha burst into tears.

William stood behind Natasha and put his arm protectively around her shoulders. "Hey, Tasha, it's okay. Everyone's safe now."

"William, she's crying." Georgia seemed to find her voice suddenly. "What were you thinking? Why on earth did you drag her back from her little trip?" She leveled a menacing glare through her one good eye. "What have you told her?"

A nurse hovered at the open door, checking on the miraculous vocal improvement in her patient.

"I'm fine," Georgia yelled at the nurse. "This conversation is private, please close the door behind you."

The young nurse raised one brow and backed out to the hallway, shutting the door quietly behind her.

"Start talking, William," Georgia ordered.

Natasha sniffled quietly and watched her father take a deep breath. He spoke in a very calm, levelheaded way in an attempt to diffuse the brewing explosion.

"Georgia, you don't realize how worried we've all been. When I couldn't get in touch with you for a couple of days, I phoned everyone I could think of in an attempt to find you. I just wanted to make sure you were okay."

"What?" Georgia squawked and flinched while holding her sore ribs. "Why would you put me through that embarrassment? What will everyone think? You gave up the right to know my whereabouts when you moved out of our house. How dare you."

"Mother," Natasha sobbed, "please stop worrying about what other people think and tell us where you've been. I know about your problem."

Silence filled the stuffy air in the hospital room. William sat down behind Natasha on the bed.

"Georgia," he said quietly, "It's time, time for honesty. Our daughter deserves to know what's going on. No more secrets. No more lies."

Natasha squared her shoulders and sat perfectly straight, bracing herself for whatever came next.

~ Fifteen ~

Georgia collapsed into the starched pillow behind her and sighed deeply.

"This is a nightmare," she mumbled. "I can't believe my life has come to this. A confessional in front of my daughter and estranged husband in a hospital bed."

"Here, Mother," Natasha said, lifting a cup of water from the side table. "Take a sip. Your throat sounds awful."

Georgia took the straw and almost drained the cup. "Thank you." She looked at her husband, who nodded encouragement.

"Okay, here goes. I've been fighting it for years, but I guess I do have a problem with alcohol. I thought I was in control, but evidently I'm not anymore. Natasha, darling, I've tried to keep it from you. We both have, for your protection. I didn't want you worrying about me, or thinking we were one of *those* families."

"One of what families?" Natasha asked, desperate to know what her mother was thinking.

"Oh, you know, the type who's rough around the edges and needy. Problem parents producing problem children."

"Mother, really? Do you honestly think there's such a thing as a problem-free family? Because I can't think of one. Some are just better at hiding the truth, that's all." Natasha looked down at her hands clasped in her lap. "We've been living a lie."

Georgia turned her head to stare at the wall and gather herself. "This sounds ridiculous, but I'm not sure where this week disappeared. I lost track of time completely and it's all rather a blur. I don't know what to tell you. I felt so incredibly down when I woke up to an empty house on Saturday, so I drank. I ended up at an all-night bar—I've never done that before."

Georgia stopped to finish the last sip of water before going on with her story.

"I checked into a hotel nearby and spent the next day in their lounge, drinking and trying to forget my mess of a life. I dreaded bumping into any of our friends, so I kept to myself. I really did."

She shot William a look of sincerity.

"I picked up what I needed at the hotel shop and went from my room to the lounge to the bar. I had a few spa treatments to relax me, but I don't think I had a clue what day of the week it was."

"You didn't think anyone would be worried? You couldn't call someone—anyone?" William asked, raking his hand through his hair.

"You were gone, Natasha was away, and quite frankly I couldn't handle any of my friends. I simply didn't care. I needed to be alone. Eventually, I must have decided to go home and that's when I crashed the car. I should never have been driving. I don't know what I was thinking."

"Mother, you could have killed yourself, or someone else."

"I know. And I'm completely ashamed about that, especially after what happened with Anita and Landon's car accident. I guess my guardian angel was looking out for me," Georgia said with a sad smile.

"Oh, you have no idea," Natasha muttered.

William reached out and gently touched his wife's hand. "Are you ready?"

She looked at him reluctantly. "Ready for what?"

"Are you ready to admit you're an alcoholic and get some real help? You know I'll support you every step of the way."

Natasha held her breath, willing her mother to agree. Seconds dragged until she thought her lungs would burst.

"Yes," Georgia whispered finally. She clutched Natasha's hand and then William's. "What have I done to us? I am sorry. Truly I am."

The most bewildering thing happened. Natasha was suddenly the strong one, stroking her mother's soft, auburn hair while tears dampened the sheets and Georgia begged her daughter and husband for forgiveness. It was a scene so unimaginable. Natasha pinched herself just in case she had fallen asleep in the car.

In a matter of minutes, Georgia's medication worked its magic and she succumbed to sleep. William grabbed the roses and left the room, muttering something about getting some water and a vase. Natasha sat and gazed at her sleeping mother.

"I have so much to tell you, Mother, so much to share. Guess I'll come back later."

She met her father in the hallway. They checked with the nurse to see what time they might return, and rode the elevator in silence again.

William put an arm around his daughter's shoulder while they exited the hospital building and strolled back to the car.

"I don't know about you, but I'm emotionally drained," he said. "How are you holding up?"

"I'm pretty exhausted," Natasha admitted. "Should we go home and rest for a bit?"

"Sounds like a good idea to me. Maybe we could pick up some of your mother's things to take back to the hospital later. I'm hoping the doctor will allow her to come home tomorrow."

Natasha drifted off to sleep a couple of times during the journey back to their house and barely had the energy to drag herself out of the car when they pulled up to the entrance.

"Why don't you go straight up to your room, Princess? I'll bring in the cases and make some tea for when you feel like it."

"Thanks, Daddy. Won't Maria be here today?" Natasha felt a sudden pang of guilt and homesickness for Mexico when she realized their housekeeper was possibly from a poor village like the one she had just left behind. She kicked herself for never really taking an interest in Maria's background before.

William opened the front door and held it for her. "I gave her a couple of days off when I knew your mother was going to be in hospital. She promised to leave some casseroles in the freezer. You go catch up on some sleep. I have a few calls to make."

Natasha dragged her legs up the spiral staircase and looked around at her opulent home. It felt weird being here again with every luxury imaginable. She missed Mexico.

Collapsing on her soft bed, Natasha uttered a prayer of thanks for her mother's safety and relatively her good physical condition, but especially for her change of heart. Her mother was softening and it might just be the fresh start they all needed.

Two hours later, Natasha felt somewhat refreshed. In an attempt to stay awake for a few more hours, she had managed to take a decent nap, quickly shower, and change into a clean pair of jeans and a black satin top.

Feeling hungry, she hurried downstairs to find her dad in the kitchen. His back was to her, but he was hunched over a legal pad and the phone.

"Hey, Tasha," he turned and sighed, managing a smile. His eyes were red-rimmed and his hair looked like he'd been through a wind tunnel.

"Who was that on the phone, Daddy? You looked totally stressed out." Natasha panicked. "It wasn't the hospital was it?"

William gave his daughter a big hug. "No. I was speaking to my lawyer about your mother's DWI charges. I think we can sort everything out. Thank goodness nobody else was hurt."

Natasha grabbed an apple from the fridge and sat on a barstool. "Oh, I hadn't even thought of that."

"Yeah, well it looks like we'll be requiring Charlie, even more than usual, if her driver's license is suspended. I'm pretty sure he won't mind."

"Perhaps you should move back home, Daddy." Natasha gave him her best puppy-dog eyes. "We need you more than ever."

William lightly pinched her cheek. "Nice try, Princess. One day at a time, okay?"

"Whatever."

~*~

Later at the hospital, the shift nurse met William and Natasha outside Georgia's room.

"Mister Smithson-Blair? I am Nurse Susan," said the middle-aged, no-nonsense woman before them. Natasha shuddered to imagine how the interactions were going between her mother and this stern matron.

"Yes? Is everything all right?" William asked.

"I'm afraid we've recently moved Mrs. Smithson-Blair to a room where we can monitor her more effectively," she replied. "She appears to have picked up an infection and her fever has spiked enough to give us concern."

"But she was fine this afternoon," Natasha wailed. She could feel her blood pumping strangely in her ears and knew she was about to faint. "I need to sit," she said quickly, collapsing onto a nearby chair.

"Honey, are you okay? What's wrong?" William asked, crouching in front of her.

"I'm feeling a little light-headed." Natasha's mouth was fuzzy and she felt the nurse pushing her head down between her knees.

"I'll get some water, dear," she said before hurrying away.

"Sorry," Natasha said from down by the floor. "I should have eaten more and I'm probably overtired. What about Mother? Can we see her?"

The nurse returned swiftly. "Let's get you back on your feet first, young lady," she said sharply. "Here, sip some water, and if you keep that down, you should drink this juice box."

Natasha did as she was told.

"Is Georgia awake?" William asked. "I mean, does she know what's going on?"

"She was sleeping when I checked on her a few moments ago," the nurse replied. "She may not be very lucid if she does wake up. We have her on some strong antibiotics and medication to get her fever reduced."

"We need to see her," Natasha announced, standing up straight. "I'm feeling better already, really I am. Please can we go now?"

"Very well, follow me." Nurse Susan led the way down the bustling corridor. "But please let her rest. Ten minutes maximum. And don't be alarmed at the monitors, dear." She directed this comment at Natasha.

"Poor Mother." Natasha rushed into the room and claimed a chair near the bed. Her father stood behind her, clearly struggling to hold it all together. Regular beeps and lights on screens screamed urgency, but Natasha felt an overwhelming sense of peace, just like the special sunrise experience in Mexico.

Instead of ranting or panicking, which she would have usually done, she bowed her head and prayed. It felt weird at first, but she silently poured her concerns out to her Heavenly Father, entrusting her mother into His loving care.

They were soon ushered to a waiting area and William wandered off to find a coffee machine and some snacks. Natasha quickly texted Bethany the latest news, asking everyone to pray again. The waiting game began. Natasha sipped coffee, had a sandwich, and napped on and off for a few hours until the nurse came in.

"Your mother would like to see you, dear," she said to Natasha. "Perhaps you could give them a few minutes, sir?"

William stood abruptly. "You mean she's okay? She's awake and everything?"

"Yes, the fever broke and it looks like we have the infection under control. Someone must have been praying."

Natasha grinned at her dad and gave him a quick hug. "Yep, that would be me. I should go and see her. Are you going to be all right, Daddy?"

"Go ahead, Princess," he said with a smile.

Georgia was back in her original room and Natasha noticed the soft, pink roses in a glass vase on the chest of drawers.

"Natasha?"

Natasha desperately wanted to go hug her mother tightly and make her promise never to take another drink again, but she knew she had to tread lightly.

She plopped on the edge of the bed and kissed her mother's warm forehead. "Mother, I have so much to tell you. I know you have a lot to tell me, too. But how about we just sit here and you rest. I'll be back in the morning, we can talk then."

Georgia, looking weaker than ever, managed a smile. "We have an awful lot to catch up on, don't we, darling?"

"More than you can imagine..."

~ * ~

The following morning, when William and Natasha arrived at the hospital, they were both relieved to see Georgia awake and looking a lot brighter than before. She'd managed to comb her hair and apply a little make-up, although the black eye was going to be a nightmare to cover up.

Natasha barely slept the previous night with the mixture of worry and fear, and felt self-conscious seeing her mother had made more of an effort with her appearance, and she was the patient.

"Mother, you look so much better," she exclaimed.

"Thanks, darling, I found the make-up bag you left on my chair and thought I should try to make myself presentable. Silly, really, with this shiner I'm sporting."

They all laughed good-naturedly and then it fell quiet.

William coughed and said, "I'll leave you girls to talk for a while. The nurse thinks you might get the green light to come home later today, so I'll check on any paperwork that needs doing."

"Sure, thank you, William. The sooner I get out of here, the better. I detest hospitals."

"Me, too," Natasha chimed in. "See you later, Daddy."

William left the room, and Natasha took a deep breath. "So, you're feeling a little better?" she asked her mother.

"Yes. Last night was all very surreal," Georgia admitted. "But it seems to me you have something you need to talk about. Is it the divorce, darling?"

Natasha shifted to get comfortable on the edge of the bed. "No, but of course I'm still worried about all that stuff. There's something else—two things actually. One I'm kind of ashamed of, and the other I'm really excited about. I'm just not sure where to begin."

Georgia took her daughter's hand and patted it. "I'm not going anywhere, Natasha. We have all morning. Take your time because I want to hear every single bit. My brush with death has given me a new appreciation for life, and I intend to do my best as a mother. I know I've done a lousy job lately, but I'm here now. I'm listening."

Natasha explained about her issues with food and her special sunrise with God in Mexico. It was odd to talk about something that had the potential to kill her one minute, and something that had given her new life in the very next breath.

But true to her promise, Georgia listened to every single word without interrupting or condemning.

Something was definitely changing and Natasha could barely contain her joy.

~ Sixteen ~

Natasha felt so full she could burst.

Not from food, that would be an ongoing battle, but at least she mustered the courage to hand that issue over to God. Her heart was full tonight and she couldn't imagine anything more perfect. All the people she loved joined together in a celebration to raise money for her friends back in Mexico, for Ricardo, the children, and for the seniors' home.

Her school for the arts had embraced the charity with open arms, especially because two of their students, Bethany and Natasha, were directly involved. Their class put together the best routines and the results were stunning. Natasha danced with every fiber of her being, as though actually performing in front of the audience of her beloved seniors and orphans.

Georgia had excelled herself. She pulled out all the stops in organizing fund-raisers, and when Natasha told her in great detail about Mexico, she used up all her favors and contacts in the city to make this event spectacular. Natasha wanted this to happen as quickly as possible and it took only a month to pull everything together. The evening was magnificent.

Even the mother-daughter relationship had blossomed since the accident and Natasha put that down to an absolute miracle. Georgia promised to help Natasha with her eating issues and had already accompanied her to several counselor appointments. Between that and her regular A.A. meetings, Natasha's mom was making every effort on the long road to recovery.

"What a night, hey?" Bethany had changed from her dance costume and bounded over to Natasha, closely followed by Todd. They had become inseparable lately, which

Natasha wasn't shocked about. It was inevitable these two were going to end up together. Still, the thought of being left behind somehow ticked Natasha off a little. She tried to push it to one side, for tonight at least.

"Hello, lovebirds," Natasha gushed. "Beth, you look amazing in emerald. And you scrub up pretty well, too, Dreamy."

"Thanks," they said in unison, and giggled.

Natasha made a face.

Bethany looked over at Georgia and gave her a quick hug. "You look so lovely, by the way." Everyone was walking on eggshells around the fragile Smithson-Blair family these days, but good old Bethany was her usual self.

"Thank you, Bethany," Georgia replied smoothly, "and this must be Todd. I'm delighted to meet you. I've heard so much about you." She put out her tanned hand, which Todd shook awkwardly.

"I've heard about you, too," he said, quickly adding, "I mean, how much effort you've put in for this fundraiser. I've never been to such a glamorous event. It's really cool."

Georgia smiled politely, but Natasha could tell it was killing her, knowing so many people were aware of her alcohol problem. This was going to be hard work, but Natasha was determined to help her through it all.

"Daddy," she exclaimed, spotting William emerging from a crowd of businessmen.

"Hey, Princess, what a night. Georgia, I have to say I think this is your best event ever. I'm proud, really I am."

Bethany and Todd disappeared toward the refreshments table, and suddenly it was just the three of them—Natasha, Georgia and William.

Her mother looked stunning in her fitted, full length, black, satin dress, yet she was jumpy and less confident than she used to be. Her injuries had healed wonderfully since the accident and only her slight hand tremors gave any clue as to what she was going through.

Her father appeared dashing in his tux, but had aged significantly these past few months. New grey hair peppered his sideburns and his eyes looked tired. No, make that exhausted. He stood near Georgia, but not with her. Natasha was praying desperately every day that their family would be reunited and whole sometime soon, but she was aware there were no guarantees.

Natasha looked from her father to her mother, wishing things could get back to the way they used to be years ago before their lives had been plagued with ugly problems. She fought the feeling of being torn between the two of them, a mother who needed her now more than ever and a father who adored her and would give her the world.

"Okay, ladies and gentlemen." Steve had the microphone and was on the stage trying to get everyone's attention. "I know I've talked way too much already." He paused while most of the youth group agreed heartily. "But we do have one more announcement before the evening draws to a close."

The hall fell silent, every eye on the pastor, who, Natasha admitted, looked like he should be on a James Bond movie set. She scanned the audience for Alice and saw her in the middle of a group of girls from the youth group. She was beautiful in a flowing deep purple gown and Natasha felt a surge of emotion for this lady. She had reacted with love and grace to Natasha's snarky comments over the years, but now Alice was her mentor, helping her in her newfound faith. How things had changed. She looked back at the stage when Steve continued speaking.

"Now, as you know, the seniors' complex down in Mexico impacted us all a great deal. We've been patching it up each year as best we can, but really the whole thing needs rebuilding and revamping. I am here tonight to tell you that work is about to happen."

Thunderous applause filled the hall until Steve was able to regain control. "Natasha, could you come up here for a minute?" he asked.

Natasha's heart pounded when she walked through the excited crowd. She spotted dear old Charlie dressed in his best suit and gave him a little wave. Subtly checking her hair was still in place in a sophisticated up-do, she made her way onto the stage. She felt her cheeks burn and was sure they perfectly matched the long, red sequined dress she was wearing.

Steve grinned and carried on with his speech. "This little lady was really touched by her time on the Mexico mission trip and when she came home, she told anyone who would listen about the plight of the orphanage and seniors' home. As I explained earlier, most of the money raised tonight will go to the orphanage. However, I'm told Natasha is a real daddy's girl and William Smithson-Blair has banded together with some of his colleagues to fund the brand new home for the seniors down in Manzanillo."

More cheers erupted and Natasha's eyes brimmed over with tears. She blew a kiss to her father and tried to compose herself in front of everyone.

"So to finish off, we have a photograph for you on this wall. It was taken yesterday." Steve turned and pointed to a large, blank wall, which was instantly filled with an image from Mexico. Natasha recognized the seniors' home, but in front of the structure was a brand new sign replacing the old rickety one.

"I hope you like the name of the new home, Natasha. Your father chose it. We happen to think he is spot on."

Tears flowed down Natasha's face, probably ruining her make-up, but she didn't care one bit. The new name was absolutely perfect. It was "*SUNRISE SENIORS*".

She ran down to her father and gave him a long hug. "How did you think of that name, Daddy?" she whispered in his ear.

William glanced over to Georgia.

"Ah, I have to give the credit to your mother for that one. We were chatting over coffee and she told me how much that special sunrise meant to you when you were in Mexico, so it seemed the obvious choice."

"Really?" Natasha looked from one parent to the other, completely blocking out the voices of other people around them. "You guys were *chatting together* over coffee? That sounds promising—"

William held his daughter's hand, and whispered, "Sunrises are so full of promise, don't you think?"

Natasha could barely breathe.

"We've got a very long way to go, darling," Georgia said softly, wiping a tear from her daughter's cheek while one trickled down her own face. "And we can't make any promises. You know how I'm surviving through this, just one day at a time."

"Yes, I understand," Natasha replied, relishing the shared tears between mother and daughter. "But you do realize I'm on speaking terms with Someone who paints the sunrise and He specializes in restoration—even for the Smithson-Blairs."

Her parents smiled while looking a little confused, but Natasha was happier than she had been in a very long time. Things weren't perfect, but she was a work-in-progress, as were her parents, and her faith was new but strong.

Tears of joy coursed down Natasha's face while she waltzed with her dad among the crowds on the dance floor. She looked up at the huge photo of the SUNRISE SENIORS sign again and she knew that tonight this was just the beginning.

Like a sunrise, her life was full of hope and promise. She was no longer torn between reality and appearances or between her father and mother. She was whole and complete—but still a princess.

Now she was a daughter of the King of Kings.

~ End ~